My body rose to hers, and I felt as if I was coming out of my old skin and into the fresh new life of her arms. Coming home, coming alive, she seared my bare defenses as her arms came around me and then her mouth found mine.

I was hungry for the taste of her but was surprised by the sound of our kiss—my heart hammering in my ears, her low moan, my startled breathing, her fingers brushing down my face. Each sound so small, but they filled me with passion as fiercely as the pressure of her mouth and the warmth of her lips.

WILD THINGS

by

Karin Kallmaker

Bella
BOOKS
2004

Bella Books, Inc.
P.O. Box 10543
Tallahassee, FL 32302

First published 1996 by Naiad Press

Printed in the United States of America on acid-free paper
First Edition

Editor: Lisa Epson
Cover designer: Bonnie Liss (Phoenix Graphics)

ISBN 1-931513-64-3

For Maria, Queen of my Heart
for all those evenings alone with a teething,
squirming child while I finished this book
And to Kelson: Moogie's done for now.

The Sixth is Serendipity

1

There is no remembrance of former things.

— ECCLESIASTES 1:11

I would have known Sydney anywhere. She had Eric's features — a square face defined by a firm jaw and a straight nose — softened with feminine curves in her cheeks. Still, I wanted to be absolutely sure, so I whispered in his ear and he nodded in agreement. His sister was seated two from the left of the podium and was in animated conversation with the woman seated to her right.

"She's lost weight," Eric whispered back.

"You needn't have been so secretive about who

your sister is," I said. Eric rolled his eyes. "You might have mentioned it sooner."

He shrugged, and I could tell he didn't want to talk about it. I also kept the tensions in my own family private. Perhaps when we left this middle stage of dating and made some sort of declaration we might talk about our families more. For now it was enough to me that he had asked me to come with him this evening as Sydney received the prestigious Roebuck Award for, as explained in the dinner program, "Dedication, Caring, and Unwavering Commitment to the Betterment of Chicago's Neighborhoods."

The program acknowledged Sydney Van Allen's many contributions to underserved areas in Chicago, including extensive pro bono representation of community organizing groups. As an alderwoman, she had written Measure D, a long overdue and narrowly approved reform of the way money is allocated among Chicago's many social and public works departments. I had voted for it and had kept that fact to myself at home, knowing that both of my parents had voted against it. She was definitely a rising star in the Chicago Democratic party. A fellow history professor had told me, and anyone else who would listen, that what this state needed was more women in the Illinois senate. Women like Sydney Van Allen. I hadn't realized until tonight that Eric was Sydney's older brother. There were a lot of Van Allens in Chicago.

The chairman of the Roebuck Foundation concluded his remarks and introduced the next speaker. I'd been to many such dinners and had already turned my chair so I could look directly at the speakers and at least appear interested in every word. Mentally, I reviewed my to-do list for tomorrow's classes and reminded myself to check with Library Services once again to see if any more of the reference books I'd requested had come in.

I interrupted my mental wanderings to applaud at the appropriate moments and then returned to my to-do list. When it was Sydney's turn to speak I gave her my full attention. I was curious about her because, for all that Sydney looked like Eric, she was the lone Democrat from a family that had voted Republican since the Magna Carta.

I glanced at Eric as she began to talk. His hazel eyes were bright, his jaw set, and his head held high. He looked as fiercely proud as a big brother could be.

"The problem with awards," Sydney was saying, "is that winning one implies someone else lost. It also implies that winning is an individual effort, which in my case couldn't be farther from the truth. Perhaps some of my hours were long. Certainly my law partners would like me to have a client I can bill from time to time." Shouts of laughter came from the table next to us. Sydney's law partners, obviously. When it died down she continued, "There were days when it didn't seem possible that anything would ever change. But then something would happen to perk me up. Like one member of my incredibly valuable staff staying up all night to research the precedent that won the Arbor Apartment Cooperative case. Or a law clerk who expected litigation experience instead offering to do safe-escort service during the blockade at Planned Parenthood last summer. And another ringing every judge in the state on a Sunday — with perfect golfing weather I might add — to find one who would sign the injunction, an act that hardly endeared him to potential future employers. So it doesn't seem right somehow to accept an award of this magnitude for work I was going to do anyway and had an amazing amount of help doing." She smiled, and I recognized the charming quirk of Eric's mouth. "But my name's on the thing so I guess I'll take it."

She spoke for another fifteen minutes, taking time to tell a brief story about each of five people she felt had made her work easier. She told funny and touching stories in a steady voice a few tones higher than Eric's low tenor.

When she finished speaking I joined Eric in standing and applauding enthusiastically. Sydney shook hands with the chairman, then her gaze sought out Eric. She smiled at him with genuine affection, then grinned as Eric bowed slightly, touching his forehead in a gesture of homage.

Eric and I took our seats again and settled in for the final speech. I had enjoyed Sydney's wit and Eric's obvious pleasure. Now bored with my unending to-do list, I studied Sydney instead. Her brown hair had hints of gold and red, just like Eric's, and her jaw, though not so pronounced, looked as if it could set into the same stubborn lines Eric's sometimes took. Her laugh was higher and seemed to come more easily than his, and her hands were long and graceful. Eric's hands were large and beefy, the only things about him that weren't elegant, and he tended to put them in his pockets whenever possible.

I studied people at the tables around us as well, looking for anyone I might know. I spotted another University of Chicago associate professor and recognized several more faces from campus, though I couldn't place them. They weren't in liberal arts, that I knew.

The last speaker concluded and, during the final, somewhat weary applause, I folded my dinner napkin and took my last look around the room. People were shrugging into suit jackets and dresses swirled, and bright chatter was filling the banquet hall. Out of all that noise and motion I saw one particular face for perhaps two seconds.

It was enough. I heard her whisper from the past, *Say that you want me.*

"Sydney, this is Faith."

"It's a pleasure and an honor," I said. I hoped that my expression and slightly clammy hands didn't reveal my churning stomach and pounding heart.

"Likewise, certainly," Sydney said. Our handshake lasted long enough to surpass mere politeness. I knew that Sydney must meet hundreds of people a week, but her warm grasp was welcoming. "I very rarely meet any of Eric's special friends."

It was a diplomatic choice of words. Eric and I were close friends. Perhaps she spoke with him enough to know we weren't lovers. I had ceased to wonder at Eric's lack of sexual demands by learning that, despite some emancipated thinking about women's roles, he was old-fashioned about sex. I appreciated that and remained quite relieved. I wasn't ready for intimacy with him.

I murmured something appropriate. My distress at the face I'd glimpsed receded under the warmth of Sydney's welcome; it did not go away entirely.

An officious-looking aide of some sort hovered at Sydney's elbow. When she finally glanced at him, he whispered something and gave Eric and me a dark-eyed glance that implied Sydney had more important people to cultivate. Sydney looked annoyed but resigned.

"Eric, if I don't mingle John the *putada* will have an aneuyism." The clean-cut man at her elbow snorted and muttered something under his breath in Spanish. Sydney glared at him and I had the feeling they interacted this way all the time. "Besides, chatting just isn't enough. Why don't you and Faith come to my place for dinner Sunday evening? Make it six and casual. It's been too long since we had a good talk."

Eric glanced at me and smiled at my eager nod. "That would be great," he said. Then, as if he couldn't help himself, he swept Sydney into his arms for a hearty embrace. "I'm so proud of you," he said. "I mean it."

Sydney had tears in her eyes when he let her go. She wished me a pleasant evening, then turned to meet two men the persistent John had ushered up to her.

Braced by Eric's protective yet undemanding hand on my back, and the affectionate exchange I'd just witnessed, I felt able to face the banquet hall. It had emptied somewhat and I kept my gaze lowered, not wanting to risk seeing that face again. I didn't want to remember or be the person I had been then.

Eric was quiet in the car and seemed content

with our comfortable silence. I was never troubled by his driving, even in the worst the Chicago highways had to offer. The Kennedy Expressway was slow but not distressingly so. I hoped he took my silence for the quiet mood of someone who had had a pleasant evening. It *had* been pleasant, with one exception.

He saw me to my door and refused my offer of coffee, as he usually did. Only occasionally did he brave the chill setting of my parents' sitting room. When he did venture inside, he went out of his way to charm them, but it took effort.

He kissed me in his usual way, with a dispassionate sweetness. Cupping my cheek, he said, "I'm glad you'll get to know Sydney. I want you to meet the rest of my family."

If my heart hadn't already been beating hard from panic, it would have leaped into double time. Meeting his family was a big step and now, my mind beginning to flood with long-buried memories, I wasn't sure I was ready. I nodded, however. "I'd like that."

I took a deep breath of the cooling night air as I watched Eric drive away.

"You're not a beautiful woman, Sydney, but I could still go for you in a big way."

Sydney favored Mark O'Leary with one of her coolest stares. The noise of the post–award ceremonies reception was only a dim clatter. "Flattery won't get you anywhere with me."

Mark didn't miss a beat. "That's the point of this little meeting, isn't it?"

Sydney turned her head slightly to look at her longtime political mentor. Alan Stevens merely quirked an eyebrow, but Sydney had no trouble interpreting his meaning. He was saying *I told you so.*

She looked back at Mark, who yanked his cigar out of his mouth and guffawed. "Well, Alan, I do believe we've unsettled the Ice Queen."

"Not at all," Sydney said. "I knew this conversation was inevitable." Mark was built like a teamster, and cigar smoking had left his teeth and hands yellow. She controlled her urge to shudder. She couldn't afford to make an enemy of Mark O'Leary. He didn't hold an official position with the Illinois Democratic party, but it didn't matter. If Mark opposed you, you were done. If he supported you, you were in. If he was tepid, you could go either way. She was aiming for tepid.

"So it's true," Mark said. The hotel guest chair creaked under his bulk. "You're a dyke."

She raised her eyebrow in a small gesture of distaste at the sound of *dyke* in his Sidney Greenstreet mouth, then nodded coolly.

"I've never understood why good-looking women go that way, have you, Alan?"

Alan shrugged. "Perhaps because you're the alternative."

Mark guffawed and slapped his knee. "That's a good one." His laughter subsided, and Sydney realized he was trying to make her think he was a buffoon. He was probably hoping she'd think she didn't need an old fool's support and tell him off.

"Gloria Steinem," Sydney said.

"You always could name a quote," Alan said. "Try

her, Mark. She can tell you where just about any quote comes from."

"That so?" Mark studied her closely for a moment. "Which are you, a dunce or a rogue?"

"Emma Goldman," Sydney said smoothly. "Her third option was an anarchist. I'm none of the above."

"Then what are you?" He made the question sound flippant, but Sydney knew it wasn't. Her answer was everything.

"I'm an ambitious woman who wants to make a positive difference in people's lives. I can play political games, but the game means nothing to me next to the end result."

"Winning?"

"Doing the right thing."

Mark grimaced at his cigar. "You're one of those do-gooder dykes."

"Whether I'm a lesbian is irrelevant. I don't intend to let it hamper me in any way."

"So you've got a nice comfortable closet."

"No," Sydney said firmly. "I am not involved with anyone and haven't been for years. I intend to keep it that way until people realize that my sexuality is both as relevant and irrelevant as the color of my skin. It influences everything I do and it influences nothing I do."

"You've lost me," Mark said, waving his hand dismissively. "I'm Joe on the street, and I don't understand a thing you've said."

Sydney lifted her chin slightly. "When it matters, it matters a lot. My thinking on civil rights is heavily influenced by my politics as a lesbian. With me so far?" Mark nodded with a frown, probably not liking her tone. "My thinking on government efficiency and spending wisely but within our means is not at all influenced by whom I sleep with. Is that clearer?"

Mark gave Alan a baleful glance.

"Don't blame it on me," Alan said. "I told you how she was. And she sees right through you, Mark."

Mark glanced sharply at her. "You think you can talk that way to me?"

"No, but I might talk that way to Joe on the street," she said sardonically.

"Not if you want to be a senator," Mark said.

Sydney couldn't control a nervous swallow. Mark saw it and smiled his terrible smile again. "Now that got a reaction. So are you telling me that I'm not gonna pump some money into your campaign only to have some big sex scandal waste it all?"

"There will be no sex scandal. However, it's possible an opponent might find out about my past relationships with women and use it. And if anyone asks me outright, I won't lie."

"You'd better learn to evade, missy." Mark's eyes took on an eerie gleam and Sydney controlled another shudder. "There are lots of people who don't want a dyke in the statehouse."

"There are already a few there," Sydney said.

"On the house side, who cares? They come and go. But senators are different. They stay. They go on to congress, they become governors and vice presidents."

Sydney leaned forward. "My life since sobriety can bear examination. The skeletons I accumulated were displayed in public when I ran for alderwoman and in the end, no one cared. Everyone knows I'm a recovering alcoholic. Everyone knows my father is richer than God and I'm not destitute myself. Inevitably, everyone will know I'm a lesbian. But by then, they will also know I don't have my hand in the cookie jar, I don't go on junkets, and I'm not trying to fuck the taxpayers or my aides."

Mark leaned back in his chair, his gaze only leaving Sydney's when he turned to look at Alan.

"If it stays that way, we can talk about the preliminary party ballot." He looked back at Sydney. "But if it doesn't, if I hear about you in anything like a compromising situation, then I'll bounce your ass out of this state."

Sydney stood up slowly. "I understand you. Understand this: I need your support, but I won't be bullied into anything. I am my own judge."

"You calling me a bully?"

Sydney realized that he was oddly pleased and felt a huge wave of relief sweep over her. "Yes. And I think you like it."

He looked at Alan and laughed. "You trained her good."

Alan stood up, and the two men shook hands. "She was born this way."

Mark stuck his cigar back in his mouth. "The winners always are."

Sydney examined her silk blouse, then dropped it into the dry cleaning hamper. Mark O'Leary would never know the amount of sweating she had done during their interview. She smiled at herself in the mirror. All she had to do to stay on Mark's good side was what she was doing already — stay focused on her law practice and political career. No distractions. She was already so good at it.

"We're in the kitchen, Faith."

The last thing I wanted was a postmortem of my evening. I needed to be alone. The wound I had thought healed needed to open and drain again. But I went to the kitchen.

I immediately sensed a family crisis. My mother had been crying and now had one hand pressed to her heart as if it were failing, which wasn't in the least likely. My father looked more grim than usual. Michael, with one arm wrapped around his chest as always, looked both stricken and annoyed.

"What is it? What's wrong?" I sat down and took my mother's hand.

Michael cleared his throat. "Abraham was in an accident and died last Friday."

I gaped at him.

My mother shook off my touch and dabbed at her eyes. "You would think that Mary Margaret would have seen fit to tell us sooner."

I bit back a reminder that my little sister had been told never to mention her husband's name in this house. A lump formed in my throat. Huskily I asked, "How did it happen?"

My father's shrug was eloquent. "A car accident was all Mary Margaret said." Obviously he hadn't asked for details.

I sighed. "How is she coping? And the baby?"

It was my mother's turn to shrug. "I don't know. I never see my grandson. Perhaps that will change."

My eyes filled with sudden tears. Meg was widowed and left with a nine-month-old baby. I had never had a chance to get to know Abraham. Meg had met and eloped with him quickly and moved almost immediately to Philadelphia where he was going to law school. She had written to me a couple of times at my office, but the anger between her and our parents spilled over to the already troubled waters between the two of us. We had never been particularly close — I had been twelve when she was born — but to be widowed at twenty-two...

"It was your choice not to see Meg. You can't blame it on anyone else." Michael snapped his mouth shut, his tone more vicious than usual. It was a by-product of being in continuous pain as the burns on his arm and chest healed.

"Let's not fight," I said, hearing the peacemaker weariness in my voice and hating both my tone and the necessity of the role. "It can't be undone now."

"She's been given another chance," my father said. "She's young. There's still time for her to marry within our faith."

I pressed my lips together, not trusting myself to speak civilly. Michael looked murderous but held his tongue as my mother pressed her handkerchief to her lips. She was shaking her head. I could almost hear the refrain in her head, *A Jew. How could she marry a Jew?* That refrain had been playing for the last two years.

Poor, poor Meg. What would she do now? Abraham's family had been only slightly more accepting of their marriage than had my parents.

13

"I'm very tired," I said, getting up.

"Tell me about your dinner," my mother said. "And Eric, I assume he is fine?" The wistfulness in her voice implied that she wouldn't have to ask if he had come in for coffee. I was devoutly grateful that he had not. I wasn't ready for him to witness firsthand the narrowness of my parents' minds. He already sensed some of it since he was a semilapsed Lutheran. My parents were Catholic right down to their DNA, and they'd passed the gene on to me.

"It was lovely. Eric was very proud of his sister. I thought she was quite . . . striking. We're having dinner with her on Sunday."

My mother's expression brightened. I was meeting some of Eric's family. It might lead to the engagement she longed for me to have. She had reminded me just last week that I wasn't getting any younger. Thirty-four was nearly a spinster, I could almost hear her thinking. I thought it myself and knew only I was to blame.

I paused long enough to give Michael's good shoulder a comforting squeeze, then finally, my heart feeling like lead, I escaped to a stinging, hot shower and my bedroom.

The first two years of my undergraduate career were the first and only time I'd lived away from home. Michael had been stationed at Fort Dearborn right in Chicago and visited frequently. If he hadn't been so close, my parents would never have consented to my living at the University of Chicago campus. After all, it was just an El ride away, there was no reason for me to be living on my own. Nice Catholic girls left their fathers' homes when they married, and for no other reason. When they married they became adults. Catholic girls who lived on their own were either nuns or whores.

But they had consented, most likely because I was joining the Catholic sorority, and I had enjoyed the first year immensely. For the first time, I began to form my own opinions and not simply repeat my father's dogmatic viewpoints. Having gone to Catholic school all my life, it was the first time I read history that wasn't pro-Catholic. I was amazed and stimulated by the different viewpoints. I'd written my first term paper in history on the difference between Catholic and feminist histories of the Inquisition.

I discovered that I was good at research and basked in praise of my writing. By the end of the year, I wanted to be a scholar. I wanted to know everything there was to know about the past, about how and why different people viewed the past differently. I discovered a hunger for information that surpassed any passion I'd ever known. For the first time in my life, I felt like an adult.

In my second year I met Renee Callahan and discovered more passions. Lust, self-loathing, dread fascination, and disgust.

That two-second glimpse of Renee Callahan across the banquet hall had brought back all those feelings. I hadn't known she had moved back to Chicago. I hadn't wanted to know. I had thought I had forgotten her and how she made me feel.

Huddled in my nightgown and shivering under the blankets, I prayed she hadn't seen me. I wanted to keep those memories behind me. I wanted instead the life Eric might offer me. But memories were churning, and I remembered the way her voice had sounded in my ear.

"Say that you want me," she had whispered.

Renee pressed me into the darkness behind the arched entrance to the Swift Hall cloister. Her hands were under my shirt and I broke out in goose pimples everywhere her fingers brushed.

"I can feel your heart beating," she whispered. "Say you want me."

I didn't want to want her. But my head was pounding and my body betrayed me again. It had betrayed me when I first met her. I had known immediately what she was and that my body was far too warm when she was near. My mind recoiled in horror even as my hands had found ways to accidentally brush hers.

"I want you," I whispered. The heat between my legs was so fierce I broke into a sweat.

She smiled in victory. I had vowed never to be with her again. And it had taken her only three days to wear down my resistance.

As she unhooked my bra, I tried to evade her for a moment. "Not here. Someone will find us."

"People have been doing just this under this arch for fifty years," she said. "Think of it as historical research." Her golden hair and skin shone platinum in the moonlight.

I wanted her to take me back to her dorm room. But she pulled up my bra and lightly caressed my aching nipples in the way that made me shudder.

"Take off your shirt," she whispered.

"No," I managed. "Please. Let's go back to your room."

"We will," she said. She pulled my shirt up and bent to me. I surged upward, offering my breasts to her. Her breath whispered over them, followed by the flick of her tongue. I whimpered and tried to push her head down, but she laughed softly. "Take off your shirt."

I had never felt so helpless. I knew she was manipulating me. I knew she had no feelings for me beyond lust. Trembling, I unbuttoned my blouse and slipped it off my shoulders.

She pinned my shoulders to the cold brick and her mouth was everywhere. She used her teeth to enhance the ache in my breasts. I pulled her against me, panting. My whimpers were gone, and I fell hard into her ocean of lust and need.

I forgot where we were. Her hand was gliding between my legs, and I staggered with the force of my response. Without hesitation I urged her inside me. I begged her in choking whispers to take me, to make me, to be in me —

I had forgotten so much. I had forgotten those blinding moments when my body had felt like fireworks.

I covered my head with the pillow and fought back tears. After the fireworks had come the loathing. I hated the weakness that had made me want her. I loathed myself for giving in to her demands. Demands that at first had seemed merely sexual had become increasingly humiliating and risky. Having sex in a public place had terrified me and she had used my newly-awakened passion to make me say I wanted her to have sex with me there. If we had been discovered she would have survived the fallout — nothing stuck to Renee and vice versa — but all my hopes

17

and dreams would have been destroyed. What if someone had found us before we were done, me half naked and her on her knees, and her mouth covered with my unmistakable desire? Why had she needed to prove she could make me do almost anything?

What would have happened if she had been as gentle as Eric, as undemanding, as kind? Would I have been filled with so much self-hate? But that wouldn't have mattered. It still would have been wrong. A sin. I knew what my parents would have done if they had known.

The only positive thing to come from the four months I had been in thrall to Renee was finally breaking free of her. Finally finding a way to say no, I had salvaged some self-respect. But not before she had proved to me beyond any doubt that I wanted her and would do almost anything to have her.

Remembering what it had been like to be with her had stirred my pulse. I might not want her any more, but I realized that I wanted passion. I told myself I would find it with Eric eventually. I promised myself. I prayed.

2

Stolen waters are sweet, and bread eaten in secret is pleasant.

— PROVERBS 9:17

As I walked through the warm haze of early fall to the train the next morning, I went through my usual school year routine, stopping in for a cinnamon bun from the bakery that was just out of sight from my parent's house. I'd been stopping in for this treat regularly since I was in my teens. Then it had been in defiance of my mother's demand that I fit into her first cotillion dress for my first cotillion — my mother always was and always will be two sizes smaller than me. She'd always bragged of a figure the same size as Jackie Kennedy's, that is until Jackie remarried. After that Jackie was never mentioned. My daily cinnamon bun was an old delicious habit with a dash of defiant memory.

On State Street I changed to the El, which would take me to Washington Park for the faculty shuttle. The uneventful ride gave me the opportunity to rest my eyes after a poor night's sleep. My thoughts turned constantly to my sister's plight. Poor Meg. What would she do now? My worry for Meg kept me from thinking about the troubling feelings Renee had reawakened.

Low clouds hung over Lake Michigan as the train emerged south of downtown along State Street. The magnificent skyline faded away to the memorials and faux Grecian colonnades of Soldier Field, then yielded to the mellow brick and ivy of Hyde Park, which was bordered on the south by the University of Chicago.

The trip south I took every weekday was a journey of extremes. From my parents' all-white neighborhood in Elmwood Park of extremely erect middle- and upper-class Polish Catholics, I traveled through the pristine Miracle Mile and Loop to the edge of Chicago's south side, where poverty and despair mix with a flair and tenacity for life that oddly pleased me. From the window of my office, I could watch the endless games of basketball and hear the laughter and fighting. It reminded me that my life was a cloistered one and there was, in fact, a world out there where people fought for survival instead of research grants.

My father called them "those people," and by that he meant African Americans, not the Polish and the Swedish Americans who also lived in the south side.

Those people, he said, only took and never gave. It did no good to ask him who he thought had done the backbreaking labor to craft Chicago's great buildings and roadways. He would have said it was the immigrant Swedes, the Norwegians, the Finns, and the Poles, like his great-grandfather. He was right, to a point. But he failed to see that all the grunt work the immigrants had not wanted to do had been put on the blacks fleeing the South, at a quarter of the wage and without benefit of union stewardship. I had certainly not seen that until I had studied history from perspectives other than the prevailing white one. As the train slowed for my Washington Park stop, I entered into a full-scale mental argument with both my parents, knowing I was stirred up because of their response to Meg's crisis.

I argued with my mother's self-righteousness. She held herself above most women because she had never worked outside the home, a sacrifice she said she had made for her children. No matter that the Altar Society and other volunteer work at the Cathedral had easily been a full-time commitment. A long string of women cared for me as I grew up — women who worked outside their own homes raising other people's children. My mother had pity and disdain for them and lived on in her fantasy of having raised three children single-handed.

I took issue with my father's story of proud immigrant stock who had had nothing when they came to America and had never received help from anyone. The only time I had ever argued with him had been over English-only laws. I had finished my first year of college and felt like I would finally be able to convince him of something. When my father said he thought Illinois should be English-only, I had answered that he was certainly lucky it hadn't been when his grandfather had arrived. When I asked how his grandfather had learned English, for his immigrant great-grandfather had never learned it, he insisted that his grandfather had picked it up on his own. I reminded him that his grandfather had learned English in a public school where the teachers spoke Polish. The Swedes had had Swedish-speaking teachers in their neighborhoods, and so on. And while sometimes the churches had held mass in Latin, everything else was in the language of the community, and the neighborhoods themselves were rightfully called little Polands, little Norways, and so on. How could he now resent little Vietnam and little Mexico and insist that only English be spoken in those neighborhood schools?

My stomach still turned over as I remembered how angry he'd been. He hadn't struck me since I was fifteen, and I had forgotten he could lose control. He shook me so hard my arms bruised. My head snapped back and I fell, but I couldn't remember if he had shoved me or if I lost my footing. He stood over me and thundered in Polish, "Remember who you are, girl!"

I remembered. I remembered, too, Meg creeping into the kitchen after he stormed out. She was only eight at the time and didn't understand that my tears were angry ones. But she learned the lesson I'd forgotten, and ever after her method of getting her way was a pretended weak and gentle disposition. She'd played the part so long she'd forgotten it was a part. The lesson I re-learned was not to argue with my father. Being an adult made no difference to his physical intimidation.

I walked briskly along the midway from the shuttle stop, arguing fitfully in my head, then turned into the first gate. As usual, my mind stilled as I felt the university claim me. Thoughts of the outside world were easy to put aside, and my mind unfailingly turned to academic matters. I could forget my family and sigh happily as I walked across the courtyard, secure with the place I had earned in the academic world.

Most of my colleagues had offices at home, but the university provided me with an office and I used it. I came to the university every weekday, regardless of when my classes were scheduled. If I wasn't teaching, attending faculty meetings, or having office hours, I did research and wrote at my computer. This quarter I only had classes Monday, Wednesday, and Friday. Since it was Thursday, I planned to get a lot of research done before I went to a radio interview.

I was just hanging up from a frustrating conversation with Library Services when James, my closest friend at work, sidled into my office with his usual smirk.

I sat back in my chair. "And today's word is?"

"*Pertinacious*," he elocuted clearly.

"My parents are pertinacious," I said. "Stubborn and perversely persistent and sometimes foolishly ignorant."

He scowled as he always did when I knew the word and straightened the framed *Vanity Fair* cover featuring Emma Thompson in armor. The imperfection of my wall hanging corrected, he dropped into my guest chair. "What do you think of this tie?"

I pondered the elegant navy silk with small but plainly discernible bananas. "I'm ape for it."

He sniffed, not willing to admit my sense of humor had any element of wit. "It's supposed to suggest that I could be peeled."

I blinked. "Who do you want to peel you?"

"No one at this third-rate institution of higher learning."

His temper was foul this morning, more so than usual. "Did they cut your teaching hours or something?"

He glared at me and didn't deign to answer. Instead, he smoothed his mustache and said, "What have your parents done that you call them pertinacious, you ungrateful child?"

I told him about Meg and that my father had actually said, with her husband in his grave less than a week, that perhaps she would marry within our faith in the future. "It's just like that whole spiel he has about his family never getting any help from anyone when they immigrated. I'm so tired of it, and every year he gets more closed-minded."

James elaborately stifled a false yawn, raised one eyebrow, and said, "How old are you?"

"Thirty-four. Why?"

"Where do you live?"

I glared at him. "Very funny. My choices are eternal damnation for leaving my father's home still unmarried or insanity from living at home."

His expression shifted from his usual hauteur to what might have been a flicker of a painful memory.

"I am going to break all my rules about giving advice."

I laughed. "You give advice all the time! I stopped wearing white stockings, remember?"

"Stocking, shmockings. That was just common sense, not advice. Same as keeping your hair short so it curls on its own. Just common sense."

"Piffle." I gave him what I hoped was a scathing glance. "What do you know about fashion?"

He returned the glance. "I'm not the one who had Marcia Brady hair until two years ago," he said crushingly. "Do you want my advice or not?"

He'd been right about the Marcia Brady hair. My current short, neatly fluffed style suited me much better. "Okay, let me have it."

"So here's my advice. Ahem. This is my advice and it is the advice I'm giving you. Ready?"

"Yes," I said patiently. When he was in this mood there was no hurrying him. Any attempt to do so would just slow him down.

He cleared his throat dramatically. "This is the beginning of my advice. Just accept the fact that you're damned in their eyes already. You need to realize you've really got nothing to lose. This is the end of my advice."

Nothing to lose. I opened my mouth to say I had plenty to lose, then closed it again. Finally I managed, "Thank you, James, it's so comforting talking to you."

He smirked and helped himself to my *New York Times*. "I'll bring you my *Trib* when I'm done. Good luck on the radio thing."

I spent the next hour thumbing distractedly through a reference book and unsuccessfully trying to make a list of what I had to lose if my parents told me never to darken their door again. At the end of the hour I'd made a few notes and citations, but my list was still blank. I felt thoroughly out of sorts as I grabbed my satchel and headed for the El again.

Thursdays are usually non-stop research days, but this particular Thursday was interrupted by an interview at the public radio station that served all the local colleges. It was based out of Roosevelt University, which was only a few El stops from me at the southernmost end of the Miracle Mile where Michigan Avenue meets Congress Parkway.

I'd done one-on-one print interviews for the alumni magazine, the student paper, and a local weekly paper, but this was my first live broadcast. The late morning was growing warm and sticky and I was glad I'd opted for cotton from the skin out. I hoped my simple shirtwaist dress wasn't too casual.

I should have worried I was attired too conservatively. The receptionist had magenta hair that made her already pale skin look deathly. She had no less than six earrings in her left ear and none on the right. Her T-shirt screamed, GET YOUR LAWS OFF MY ASS.

She spoke very fast and with no audible forms of punctuation. "I'm so glad to meet you I just loved your book I can't wait to hear you Liz is waiting in the studio follow me this way turn here I'll bring water."

She continued with her breathless tour through a maze of desks, some with cubicles but most back-to-back and occupied by at least one and sometimes two people. Everyone wore jeans and political T-shirts, and loud conversations in a variety of languages assaulted my ears. The entire station was atremble with the righteous vigor of people working for a cause.

To my relief, Liz, who had called me for the interview, turned out to be in her mid-forties and as interesting as she had sounded on the phone. Her voice had the rich warmth that many large black women's have, and she spoke with a depth of thought and clarity that made me want both to talk and listen.

"I'm so glad we're finally going to do this interview," she said, pushing back a mass of black curls that had escaped from a beaded bandeau. "I wanted to do it after your first book, but the schedule was so full and the river just keeps on rolling by, doesn't it?" She was wearing a light, fragrant attar of rose, and the small studio was cool and soothing, like a flower shop.

"I know what you mean. The quarter starts, then it's time for finals and then I have new students. It's only the middle of September and my summer trip to France seems like a year ago."

We chatted while she pointed out the various lights that would tell me when we were live and showed me how to damp my microphone if I had to sneeze or cough. By the time our hour began I was relaxed.

"I have a dictionary of quotations by women," Liz said when the LIVE sign turned red, "and in it Eleanor Roosevelt, of course, is listed. I found it curious that not one word of her bio mentioned that she was married — or to whom. I thought that this took political correctness a little too far. She was a citizen of the world in her own right, and much of her life's work was hers and hers alone. Still, there's no way to divide Eleanor from Franklin, and in so many lives of powerful and famous women, the same is true. And that's what I'm going to talk about with my guest today. Say hello, Faith."

"Hello," I said, then gratefully realized that she did this to let me get my first word out without it having to be an important one.

"Faith Fitzgerald has written fictionalized biographies of two remarkable women whose lives, while being inseparable from the men of their times, have a light of their own that shines past the surrounding men. For example, I have found it exceedingly tedious that every biography of Elizabeth the First of England details endlessly whom she might have married, whom she might have slept with, and which men had the greatest influence over her at what times."

"A perfect example," I interjected. "I think I would have tackled Elizabeth if there weren't already hundreds of biographies available."

"Instead, you chose another English queen, Maud."

"Not everyone agrees she was ever queen," I reminded her.

"As your book so clearly points out. For the listeners, Faith's first book, *Maud*, detailed the twelfth-century struggle for control of England which Empress Maud — sometimes called Matilda — almost won. It portrays how Maud's own strength of character is what kept her struggle going, while all the visible action, especially the warfare, was masterminded by her brother. Faith's latest book is *Isabella* and I found it stunning."

In her pause, I said, "Why thank you. I take that as high praise."

"What is it about these women that made them so compelling for you?"

"When I was a lowly undergraduate I was infected by history. I majored in it, I lived it, I read it every chance I could." I laughed a little and added, "It won't surprise anyone if I say I found the mention of women's influence on history completely missing or stated only as a conduit or background for the male activities."

"What a shocker," Liz said dryly. "I can hardly believe that's true."

"Oh, it's true," I said, equally droll. More briskly, I went on, "What I noticed about many influential women in history was that they had economic resources. Maud was heir to several principalities, including Britain. Isabella was queen of two countries, and that's how she financed Cristóbal Colón's expedition."

"That's what struck me so vividly about Isabella," Liz said. "You portray her financial backing as a business decision, not as a romantic indulgence to a young, adventurous lover."

"There are historians who don't agree with me," I said, my tone now dry. "They would prefer to portray Colón as the dynamic lover who talked Isabella into giving him her jewels secretly. I don't know why her financing Colón would have been a secret. Isabella wasn't some country maid fortunate enough to marry the king of Spain. She was queen of Castile and León. Ferdinand was the king of Aragon. Together they unified Spain. She seized control of the military religious orders and took the Inquisition under royal influence. She administered law in her own lands. She was a brilliant strategist and knew how to take risks. It's so frustrating to read children's Christopher Columbus books and have her referred to unfailingly only as Ferdinand's wife. Her own titles are never mentioned." I realized I was running on and talking too fast. "Anyway, the funds she used to finance the expeditions were from her own lands and income. Ferdinand had turned Colón's request for money down. Colón didn't skulk off and beg money from Isabella, he applied to her as queen of Castile in open court — her court."

"You don't portray Colón as Isabella's lover."

I smiled. "Maybe he was, but I doubt it. Isabella was a devout Catholic, and one of the outcomes of her faith was the Inquisition. She had no qualms about having people tortured and killed. But she was never referred to by anyone as a hypocrite. She publicly decried adultery. I think she practiced what she preached. Spain was a violent place close to the Holy Land, and religion was a violent matter."

"It still is," Liz said archly.

"You're quite right," I acknowledged. "Other biographers argue that her religious fervor would not have stopped her from taking a lover. She was, after all, an aristocrat. She could buy her reputation if need be. In that regard she is the same as the woman in the book I'm currently working on, Eleanor of Aquitaine."

"I can't wait," Liz said, her eyes widening with interest. "Talk about daring women! Let's come back to her at the end of the program, because I'm not ready to leave Isabella." She sipped her water. "You made an interesting choice of narrators for the story."

I nodded, then realized only Liz could see me. "One of the difficulties of telling Isabella's story is that the bold risk she took in backing Colón financially led to the European invasion of this continent. Colón's expedition was audacious and inspired, and Isabella's decision to back it changed the world forever. She financed an adventure of unprecedented magnitude. It also unleashed one of the most vicious and prolonged periods of genocide in the history of the world. I couldn't tell the story without that perspective."

"Did she really see it as anything more than a business gamble?"

"It's difficult to know for sure. Yes, she gave Colón money. Sooner or later someone would have. But in the end, hundreds of thousands of North and South American natives died in the following two hundred years because Isabella was hoping to make a profit. So I wanted my narrator to know that bitter fact, and yet be drawn to admire her namesake ancestress for her vision, and her daring, and her wits."

"And in so doing," Liz added, "you told the story of a modern woman involved in an adventure of her own."

"That's why it's called fictionalized history," I said with a laugh. "The modern Isabella didn't really exist. But I needed her to explain the bittersweet context."

Liz smiled encouragingly. "That was another aspect of the book that kept me reading. The story of two Isabellas: the queen hoping to strike it big with trade to India by sea, and the biochemist working on a cure for the smallpox her ancestress was responsible for bringing to this continent."

I leaned a little closer to the microphone. "Smallpox was more deadly than swords and guns in the end."

"Tell me more about Eleanor of Aquitaine," Liz said. "I find her so fascinating as a character. It's hard not to see Katharine Hepburn whenever I think of her."

I smiled. "I know what you mean. Katharine Hepburn played her so well in *The Lion in Winter*. That portrayal of Eleanor makes wonderful theater. If anything, I'm struggling with too much material and a personality so vivid it's hard to capture her on the page. Existing biographies are usually of the Eleanor-and-the-kings-in-her-life variety — more about the kings' reactions to her than her own actions. I'm hoping to do better than that since she deserves it."

"Which is where we began. You can't tell the story of her life without all the kings she influenced in it."

"Certainly not," I said. "But I can make Eleanor the center of my biographic universe and show how her wit and intellect influenced all she touched, not just her beauty and the passion men had for her. *The Lion in Winter* portrays Henry's feelings for her as either hate or love. She had to have been more than a bed companion to him or a hated enemy. She did more than simply madden him — and everyone else around her — into irrationality."

"I begin to see what you mean," Liz said. "I can't

think of any portrayal of her that doesn't center on how she drove other people mad with lust or hate, as if to say that as a woman she worked only by arousing strong emotions in men, but that can hardly be the case."

"And showing that is what I'm hoping to accomplish in the book."

Liz glanced at her watch. "Why don't you leave us with a brief synopsis of her life so when your book is on the stands we'll know why we want to read it."

I took a deep breath. "What fascinates me about her is what she had from birth and what she did with it. She was heiress to one of the richest agricultural centers in Europe, almost a quarter the size of modern-day France. It was hers and hers alone. Her father was mostly absent and left her active mind to its own devices. At fourteen she could speak langue d'oc, which was the language of the Aquitaine, court French and classic Italian, as well as read and write in Latin. When I was fourteen, I was listening to 'Frampton Comes Alive'."

Liz chuckled. "I was busy learning all the words to 'Alice's Restaurant'."

I shared her laughter. "We were still children, but Eleanor was already considered an adult by her fourteenth birthday. She was the darling and star of a circle of women who set the code of medieval conduct. They were the first to look back at the Arthurian era and immortalize it in verse. Most history texts comment on the sudden rise of music and art and the spontaneous development of chivalric behavior by knights, but few go out of their way to point out that women shaped these changes. The women created a culture that would influence European thought for three hundred years."

"The women were the cultural influence?" Liz leaned forward with an intrigued expression.

"Unquestionably. They demanded that a knight be more than a warrior. He must have an appreciation of beauty, of poetry. He must at all times keep his temper and, above all, revere and protect women and the weak. He must be in touch with his feminine side, if you will." I laughed. "The penalty for crudity of any kind was ostracism by the ladies."

"I'm intrigued," Liz said. "Those were barbaric times."

"Absolutely. For example, a high-born heiress like Eleanor had to have an armed escort of knights because it was common for lords to ambush such women, carry them off, and either threaten or commit rape to force a marriage. No matter how he managed to get her to the altar once it was done her property was his. Her children would be his. Though her family or betrothed husband might take vengeance through war, the property was lost forever."

Liz was shaking her head. "And all anyone really cared about was the property."

"Precisely," I said. "Property and money. And local wars ruined only the peasants because burning their crops and homes was one way to win a war. But by the time the chivalric code was entrenched, the rules of conduct for upper class society had changed forever. This renaissance of civilized behavior was the direct result of educating a certain class of women and then leaving them alone. Men had been going off on crusade for the last fifty years, and when they left town, the women ran things. Castellans and seneschals fortified castles and saw to harvests, but the women set the tone of governance and sometimes sat as judges in the absence of their husbands. This was the world that Eleanor was born into. She was the richest young woman in a society where women had more cultural influence than ever before, a society that saw itself as the pinnacle of civilization with the glory of God on its side. She was already so high in social class that at sixteen she took the only step up available to her — she married the king of France."

"And ended up married to the king of England — Maud's son. But her first husband didn't die, did he?"

"Oh no. Eleanor was a divorcée when divorce could only be purchased directly from the pope. At the age of twenty-seven — when I was just beginning to live an adult life after college — she evidently decided to start over with hers. She didn't want to be queen of an already complete society. She was lured by the wild thing needing to be tamed. In this case, Henry Plantagenet, Duke of Normandy and ten years her junior. He had prospects of being England's next king. To a Norman-French woman, England was a barbaric place, badly in need of refinement."

"A challenge in a dull life," Liz said. "So she divorced her boring husband and married the barbarian."

I was nodding. "Exactly. She spent a fortune buying that divorce from the pope. The abbés, who guided the naive king of France, were eager to be rid of a headstrong queen who had failed to give the crown sons. She bought the divorce and went after

Henry, the forbidden, wild thing. She gave up the Aquitaine to Henry as her dowry and had eight children, four of them boys. Her attempts to raise England to a height of political power and culture that would eclipse France shaped British history for two hundred years. But things didn't go exactly as she had planned. Henry was a far stronger man than Louis. And when it was clear to her that Henry would never give her the power she wanted, she asked for the Aquitaine back. He said no, so she raised an army against him."

"I like this woman," Liz said with a laugh. "She didn't take no from anyone, did she?"

"Her husband and sons found it frequently necessary to detain her under guard."

Liz chortled. "How priceless."

"That's the spirit I want to catch. Rather than painting her a gnat those great men had to swat at occasionally, I want to show what a monumental pain in the backside she was for them when they ignored her, both politically and personally. She saw her first son, Richard Lion-Heart, crowned king of England. She considered him unfit, that is he took other people's advice over hers, so she imprisoned him for many years and ruled in his place. He was a homosexual, too, and had no heirs. So her next living son, John, followed Richard onto the throne."

"That would be the evil Prince John of Robin Hood fame?"

"The very same. John is the also king who signed the Magna Carta, which was the culmination of the intellectual revolution that Eleanor was a part of. The rights John gave to his nobles that day were the very rights that Eleanor, as a woman, had struggled for all her life. Foremost among them was an inalienable right to participate in the political process and seek justice above the King's word."

"I can tell I'm going to love this book," Liz said with a sparkle in her eyes.

"Well, I don't want to make Eleanor seem a feminist! Yes, she struggled for those rights, but she thought they were her due because of her social class. She hated the Magna Carta because it elevated the rabble. So I have a challenge, as you can see. It'll be about two years before *Eleanor* is in print, and only then if I get cracking. It's hard to know where to begin," I said. "I hope everyone can wait."

Liz thanked the listeners and me, then the OFF AIR sign came on.

"That was fun," I said, meaning it. "You made it very easy."

"So did you," Liz said. "I could have talked all afternoon. For once I felt like the callers were getting in the way."

Two men rushed into the studio and hustled Liz and me out. As we were herded into the corridor, Liz apologized for our peremptory removal. "I forgot that the other studio has a bad mike. Listen, I'm having a party tomorrow night and some of my local writer friends will be there, as well as a few other women notables. Would you like to come? I think you'd enjoy yourself. I know several of my friends would enjoy talking to you."

I said yes with pleasure and took down Liz's address. She assured me I didn't need to bring anything, but I made a mental note to leave enough time in the evening to pick up some flowers or wine. I took leave of her and walked to the El station as briskly as the humid afternoon would allow.

On the short ride back to the university, feeling a pleasant glow from the success of the interview, I remembered James's challenge to realize that I had nothing to lose in my relationship to my parents. Perhaps that's why, as soon as I got to my office, I dialed Meg's number. She was not anathema to me, even if our relationship had had its tense moments.

Her voice was wan, and I could hear a baby crying — David, my nephew.

"Meg, it's Faith."

"Faith," she repeated. There was a long silence. Then I heard her swallow noisily and knew she was crying.

"If you had called, I would have come," I said around a tight knot in my throat. "I still can."

"No," she said, after clearing her throat. "I don't need you — not right now," she said more quietly, taking the sting out of her words.

"Tell me what I can do," I said.

"You can send me a plane ticket," Meg said. "Abe's life insurance won't pay for another two months and I had to spend what we'd saved on the funeral. I won't take money from his parents. Or Mom and Dad."

It was a small comfort that Meg would take money from me. "Where do you want to go?"

She sniffed. "I don't have any choice. I've got no

way to pay the rent and the student subsidies died with Abe. I'm coming home for a while."

"Do Mom and Dad know?"

"No, but I have a secret weapon, and that's David. They won't leave their grandson, even if he is half Jew, on the doorstep." David let out a squall as if to confirm his powers of persuasion. Meg said, "I've got to go. Will you front me some cash? I want to get out of here by Monday. I was going to call you today. I really was."

"Of course," I said. "I'll send a cashier's check by overnight mail. Meg, I'm so sorry."

David's cries were increasing in volume, but I heard her say "So am I" before she hung up.

Meg was right, my parents would never shut David out of their house. If they let him in, Meg had to come too.

Then I realized that all of us would be under the same roof again. We'd grown up, but I didn't want to fall back into childhood roles. I had a hard enough time with the adult ones.

James slipped into my office, startling me out of my daze.

"Sleeping with your eyes open again?"

"I just had the most civil conversation with my sister I've had in over two years."

"Death will do that," he said cynically. "I wouldn't take it as a predictor of future behavior."

"I won't," I said slowly. "Or maybe I will. I don't know. She's coming home . . ."

James snapped his fingers and I started. "You *are* alive. I thought you were an amazing simulation."

I gazed at him for a moment. "Do you get on with your parents?"

"Not in the least," he said. He fiddled with the end of his tie. "We haven't spoken since the last family funeral, as a matter of fact."

"Humph. What did it feel like, when you finally went your separate ways?"

"I remember a long, dark passage with a bright light at the end. Finally, I reached the light. Then someone slapped me on the butt."

"Be serious," I said, frowning.

He took offense. "I am *always* serious. And I've always been on my own. About eight years ago I decided not to pretend anymore. I can't say I've missed them."

"What made you an outcast?"

When he didn't say anything, I retracted the question. "Sorry, that was too personal, wasn't it?"

"Someday," he said very seriously, "I will tell you all about a lifetime of being vaguely normal. Here's my *Trib*. Dilbert's quite apropos today."

"Thanks," I said as he shrugged into his backpack with a wince. "That looks heavier than usual."

He sighed and prodded his side as if it hurt. "It's full of assistant professor type work. Something an associate professor wouldn't know anything about."

"You're not going to make me feel guilty about getting tenure. And I'm still teaching in the college, no graduate seminars or anything so exciting as that." He'd been trying to make me feel guilty since the beginning of the quarter.

"I should have chosen history. Less competition than English." He grunted as he tightened the backpack straps.

"That's a laugh. It was sheer luck it opened up and sheer luck I got it."

James favored me with a sullen glare. "If you had half an ego I'd enjoy deflating it."

"I do so have an ego," I protested.

"How old are you?"

"Thirty-four, and I know where I live, thank you very much," I snapped. James could be so aggravating sometimes.

"See you on Monday," he said and I watched him stride down the corridor.

I looked down at the *Tribune* he'd left me and discovered he had folded the apartments-for-rent section so it was the first thing I'd see. The vertically-challenged interfering little so-and-so.

3

He that curseth his father, or his mother, shall surely be put to death.

— EXODUS 21:17

Sydney hummed along with Tracy Chapman's "Talkin' Bout a Revolution" and grinned as Cheryl looked at her over her glasses. "I do get out sometimes, you know."

Cheryl raised her precisely defined eyebrows. "Yeah, boss. As if that song isn't ten years old. You want me to tell Gina to turn it down again?"

Sydney shook her head and glanced at her watch. "It's after seven. She's good enough to stay, so let her enjoy her music. Tell me we're on the last item."

"We are. Mark O'Leary wants you to come to a private dinner, just twenty people or so. Next Wednesday at eight."

Sydney started to shake her head. "I've got . . . I suppose I can postpone the ALP dinner meeting. Or they can go ahead without me. Confirm that I'll be there."

.Cheryl made a note, then looked at her over her glasses again. "Is Mark O'Leary cultivating you?"

Sydney was annoyed for a moment, then reminded herself that at least six other attorneys had tried to hire Cheryl away from her in the last year alone. "Let's just say I'm willing to be cultivated, but not plowed."

Cheryl snickered in her prim way. "Have you made up your mind? Are you really going to run? I've never been a senator's assistant."

"I haven't been given the go-ahead to run for it —"

"As if you've ever waited to be asked for anything," Cheryl said, a fond smile etching deep lines in her olive-toned skin. She smoothed her meticulously knotted scarf.

"Well, Mark O'Leary isn't opposed to the idea, which means I can at least consider it."

"He's not a nice man," Cheryl said. Nice was a virtue to Cheryl.

Sydney thought that was an understatement. "I wouldn't wear a belt around him — it would only give him a better chance of hitting you below it."

"You sure you want to go to his dinner?"

"I want him to leave me alone. I think he'll have to get to know me better to see that I really do mean it. So I'll go."

Cheryl flipped her notepad shut and neatly threaded her precisely sharpened number 2 Ticonderoga through the wire spiral. Sydney tried not to smile. Cheryl's action signaled that as far as she was concerned, the day was over. In the morning she'd remove the pencil, resharpen it precisely, and open the pad to start the day.

"I would stay," Cheryl was saying, "but Mr. Fluffy has to have his bath tonight."

"You're the only person I know who bathes her cats. Lord knows Duchess could use one, but I wouldn't live to tell."

"She doesn't know who the human is and who the cat is," Cheryl said. Cats were a serious business to her.

"She knows full well who the cat is, she just refuses to acknowledge any change in cat status since Egypt."

"You spoil her," Cheryl said from the doorway. "See you in the morning."

Sydney went back to editing her brief and found herself humming to Gina's tape. This time it was Melissa Etheridge. Gina couldn't spell worth a darn, but she had good taste in music. She called out, "How's it going, Gina?"

The reply came back muffled. Gina was probably having a Snickers. "Fine. I'll have the first ten pages done in another five or so."

Sydney picked up the papers she had reviewed and took them to Gina, who was indeed eating a Snickers as she huddled over her keyboard.

"Here's the next ten pages or so. Have a bite?"

Gina handed her the candy bar without looking up. "You shoulda had dinner."

Sydney savored the chocolate. Sometimes it made her feel almost as good as Glenfiddich used to. "I should have had lunch, too."

Gina glanced at her, then said, "You don't need to lose an ounce, you know. I think you're perfect, not that you've ever noticed."

"Gina . . ." Sydney sighed. "Let's not start that discussion again, okay?"

"Okay," she said. "I have a new gal, you know. So you're safe, girlfriend." She glanced up, her dark eyes twinkling. "At least for now."

"Gina, you're a flirt," Sydney said, walking back to her office. She heard Gina mutter "And you're an icebox" and knew Gina meant her to hear, so she didn't respond in kind. Gina was harmless, but even a little light banter could be misinterpreted — not by Gina, but by anyone else still working in the office.

As she picked up the next page of the brief, she remembered Gina's attempt at seduction. Gina would never know that Sydney had been tempted, just like she was tempted to have a drink at least once a week. But Sydney didn't give in to such temptations any more. Drinking had almost cost her her life and her family. An affair could cost her the dreams she had cherished for the last eight years.

"What starts a revolution?" I glanced at my students, noticing that I had, as usual, the attention of about two-thirds of the class. "Come on, it was your reading assignment. I'll make it easier. What started the French Revolution?"

Guesses ranged from a nobleman running down a

street urchin with his carriage (Victor Hugo, apocrypha), to a new tax (factual), to a particularly spectacular and wasteful party thrown by the aristocracy (probable). Starvation, poverty, disease, imperialism, exploitation, child labor, too many writing assignments, and general misery were also suggested. Then the more involved students, of which thankfully there were a half-dozen, began to lump causes together.

"It's not just one thing," said the only student in class who showed flashes of passion for the subject. "It's a lot of little things until finally one more — even something silly — is just too much to bear."

Their assignment for Monday, met with groans, was to create a table to compare and contrast the causes of the American and French Revolutions. It was only noon, but I resolutely left my office and got on the El, armed with the *Tribune* apartments-to-rent section.

What starts a revolution? What prompted Eleanor, married five years to Louis of France, to make her first appeal for divorce on the basis of consanguinity? Louis had been a second son and had trained for the church. Had she finally realized she had married a monk, not a king? Had she become utterly bored with the dullness of Louis's court, finding it empty of direction and intellectual pursuits? It mattered very little because the same abbés who found her not too closely related to Louis for marriage found so again. Eleanor stayed married to Louis, at least for a while longer.

A revolution — even a personal one — does begin from a lot of little things. For me those little things were deeply buried memories surfacing again. Not just Renee Callahan, but what life had been like before Meg left home.

As the El clacked towards North Avenue, I thought about what it would be like to see Meg every day and spend my evenings trying to make peace between her and our parents. It had always been my role and I didn't want it again. Meg and I got along better on our own. Meg's coming home, even for a few months, seemed like a sign to me. It was time to conquer some territory of my own.

I had spent the previous evening looking at my bankbook and playing with a budget. Today I studied my bankbook again until the El stop near Lincoln Park. I had paid off my student loans ahead of schedule by applying all of my previous royalties to the balance. My paycheck over the last few years had helped with household expenses and had finally paid off my parents' mortgage. Now I was free of debt, had an advance for *Eleanor* and a substantially increased paycheck because I was tenured. The only large sums of money I spent were on travel, and I needn't go to Europe again next summer. There was no economic reason to live at home. I thought about where my relationship with Eric might lead, but decided that was irrelevant to today. I had to think about now, not what might be. That left the larger reason — honoring the traditions of my parents and our church.

I told myself that if Joan of Arc had lived to be thirty-four, she wouldn't have lived at home either. Of course I was no saint. Despite my intentions to relegate Renee to the back of my mind, I had dreamed about her last night and woke up in a sweat. *Say that you want me*, I could hear her whispering. The memories of my anguish made my head throb. I had thought I was over it. I wanted to be over it and over her. But when I finally slept again, I dreamed once more, but this time only of sex. Sex and Renee, and my body so tightly tuned to her that she played me in her own symphony.

I had awakened just after daybreak in a different kind of sweat and found myself reaching for James's too-tempting apartments-for-rent listings. I couldn't stay in the house with my long-choked anger, not with Meg and a baby and Michael who spent all his time either indifferent or angry. I needed space. The baby could have my room.

Looking for an apartment was my act of revolution. Millions of children finally step away from their parents and live to tell. Meg and Michael had both done it. Well, Michael was a man and that made a difference to my parents. Meg hadn't even looked back, but she was younger and, somehow, accommodating Meg became important for everyone around her. My parents had always tried not to upset Meg rather than the other way around, she being of a delicate, ultrafeminine constitution. I was made of sturdier stuff. My father might hit me, but I would survive.

Renee had nothing to do with my feelings of being closed in and trapped. I told myself this lie, knowing it was a lie, over and over. But the way my body felt after thinking about her — I couldn't understand it and I didn't want it. Nor did it help to think of Eric. I was having trouble thinking at all. My life had been so orderly until I had seen her again. And now everything seemed to be happening all at once: Eric, Meg, Renee and feelings that just wouldn't go away.

Lincoln Park was a nice, collegiate area, and I found myself writing a check for first month's rent and security deposit for an apartment on Menominee, just a few blocks from the El. Close transit was important because I didn't want to buy a car. Cabs would still be affordable for me after dark. The apartment was in an older building and would get bright morning sun. The hardwood floors creaked pleasantly, and the lake breeze would pass through its three rooms: large living room, tiny kitchen and bedroom a little larger than I was used to. It suited me perfectly, and I could move in right away.

My next stop was a furniture store where I purchased a bedroom set, a big computer desk, living room furniture, and two large rugs, all for delivery the following Tuesday. I indulged my love of soft blues and purples in everything I picked out. Cookware and other essentials I could acquire by catalog when I felt the need for them. In less than three hours I had completely changed my life, and I had enough time left to buy a bouquet of tiger lilies to take to Liz's party.

As I approached the house where I had grown up, I braced myself for the inevitable. It was childish, but helpful, to imagine I was Eleanor, Duchess of Aquitaine, Countess of Poitou, Queen of France, Queen of England, who would not for even one moment have allowed anyone to question her choices.

I waited to make my announcement until the dinner dishes were done, my father had finished his after-dinner whiskey, and we were all settled in the kitchen.

My parents were shocked into silence, but Michael said heartily, "Good for you!" I sent him a grateful smile, and for a moment he looked like the old Michael.

"Now wait just a second," my father said, his already florid face reddening. "I absolutely forbid it. What will people think?"

"They'll think I'm thirty-four, with a good job of my own, and am capable of standing on my own two feet."

My mother, one hand pressed to her heart as always during crisis, said, "It's because of Eric, isn't it?"

"No, it has nothing to do with Eric."

"But he'll visit you, won't he," she persisted suspiciously.

"Of course he will."

"A good Catholic boy would visit you under your father's eye," my father pronounced. "You'll turn out just like Meg."

"Leave Meg out of it," I said, my voice rising. I would not argue about whether her marriage to a Jew was tantamount to living in sin. "I am not Meg. I will make my own mistakes. But I am moving out. On Tuesday."

My mother's breath caught and for a moment she looked sad.

"It's okay, Mom, I'll come by all the time. For Sunday Mass, too." I patted her hand.

She slid it out from under mine. "If you're doing anything shameful, don't bother."

Michael, hugging his bad right arm against his side, said softly, "Be careful, Mom. It cuts both ways."

"No," she said sharply. "If your sister insists on doing this thing, then she must take the consequences. This Eric is not a nice boy like I thought. Lutherans . . ." She spat the word in much the way she spat the word *Jew*.

Michael muttered just loud enough for me to hear, "Like I can't name six popes who killed people."

"Mom, I'll be okay," I said patiently, trying not to laugh at Michael. "I'm not moving in with him."

"This is not funny, young lady. And you'd better not be living in sin," my father said. His voice deepened as he summoned up his worst tone of condemnation. "I would rather see you dead than a tramp."

I stared at him and slowly stood up. "At least now I know what thirty-four years of obedience have gained me. Nothing. I move out and now I'm a tramp?"

"Why else would you want to leave the protection of your father?"

"I'm a professor now," I said passionately. "I'm a full-grown woman."

"He only wants one thing," my mother said. "You won't get a ring from him."

I exploded with rage I hadn't let surface for years. "I'm doing this for me," I shouted. "I want to live in the twentieth century!"

"Faith Catherine Fitzgerald!" My mother was on her feet now. "You won't speak to your father in that tone. I won't have it."

I gritted my teeth and said, "I will not let him

call me names simply because I want to be independent."

"Maybe we are old-fashioned," my mother said, with a hurt sniff. "Perhaps you would have preferred we ignore our responsibilities. I never had the chances you've had, I had babies to take care of, and I was the wife of the head usher of St. Anthony's Cathedral. We do what we must, and I won't have you criticize me for it."

I softened my tone. "I'm not criticizing you. I'm just saying I'm old enough to be my own keeper."

"I forbid it," my father said.

I turned from my mother's pained, accusing glare to confront my father. Michael was pale. He watched the exchange like someone at a tennis match being played with grenades. Since his accident he hadn't cared enough to argue about anything.

"You can't stop me," I said slowly. "You might as well accept it."

My father shoved a kitchen chair aside in his rush across the room toward me. I was prepared for his enraged blow. When he hit me, it would be proof that my leaving was justified.

"Thomas, no," I heard my mother gasp. She had never protested before.

I stood my ground. I thought irrelevantly that Eleanor would have had him put to death for merely approaching her with his fist raised. There was something to absolute power.

Michael got there first. He pinned him against the counter for the few seconds it took for our father to regain his control, before letting himself be shrugged off. Michael was white with pain.

My father towered over me. "Get out of my sight! Pray God I forgive you."

I walked away on legs of rubber, not out of the room, but to put one arm around Michael. "Are you okay?"

He nodded tightly.

"I'll run a cool bath for you," I offered. It was a small service, but he knew I was trying to thank him. We went out of the kitchen together, leaving behind a stunned silence.

Michael leaned heavily on me as we went up the narrow stairs and didn't seem to notice how badly I was shaking. "What do you do for an encore?"

"I go to a wild party and stay out most of the night," I said. I felt him shudder with laughter and realized I hadn't seen him laugh in ages.

"Good for you," he said again. "Do you think if I were healthy I'd be living here?"

I pushed open the door to his room and started to help him inside.

"Nah," he said, pushing me away. "I'm okay. It just hurts so damn much."

"You let your painkiller prescription run out again, didn't you?"

He shrugged. "I don't want to get addicted. Though they tell me kicking the addiction hurts less than the skin grafts. Still, I'm trying to tough it out."

I pursed my lips. Michael was getting good care from the Navy, but I found his stoicism foolish. Still, I wasn't the one who had crawled out of an engine-room fire and lived to tell of it.

"You want that cool bath?"

"Sure," he said. As I turned away he said, "Hey, Ensign . . ."

"Yes, Lieutenant?" I turned back.

He gave me a little salute. "Chin up, sailor."

"Aye, sir."

Chet Baker's creamy voice, crooning "Let's Get Lost," streamed past Liz when she opened her door. I was still shaking inside, feeling a little drunk with the enormity of stepping into a future I had never envisioned. Liz's smile and warmth made me feel a lot less terrified.

"These are so beautiful," Liz said, taking the lilies from me. "I love fresh flowers. I'll put them in water, then introduce you around."

Her top-floor flat in the three-story building was overflowing with women. I was glad I hadn't asked Eric to come with me. Not only would it have been presumptuous, since Liz had not mentioned bringing a guest, but he would definitely have felt out of place.

The shaky feeling went away, and I felt a flooding rush of confidence and happiness fill me as Liz took me from group to group. I met several women who had read one of my books and was soothed by their genuine praise. My parents thought my condemnation of the Inquisition in *Isabella* was borderline heresy and gave me only criticism. In the scheme of publishing by professors at a university with more than fifty Nobel laureates to its credit and over twelve hundred full-time faculty, my books were distinctly small potatoes. They sold rather well, but didn't show up on best-seller lists. The praise of other writers and academics pampered my bruised ego, and I was very glad Liz had invited me.

She finally left me in conversation with an older woman with attractive gray streaks in russet hair. Nara Rogier had just published a photo essay of gargoyles. As she left us, Liz grinned at me as if to say, "I knew you'd enjoy yourself."

Nara and I swapped what-were-you-thinking-when-you-saw-the-altar-at-Notre-Dame stories, then moved on to other French and English gothic structures and the ideas and images they had stirred for us.

"The Tower of London made me dizzy," Nara said, her eyes shining. She hadn't lived in Ireland for years, but her voice still carried a soft lilt that made her words almost musical. "I walked through Traitor's Gate and thought of all the people who had done that before me. The grounds where they erected the executioner's scaffolds — I was thinking of Anne Boleyn and how she apologized to the executioner for her small neck. And four centuries later I was standing in exactly the same place that she died. I was sobbing like . . . oh, like I did when Beth died in *Little Women*. I felt it so personally. Old places do that to me."

"Me, too," I said. "When I went outside Notre Dame and walked around the plaza, I started thinking about all those people who came for Henry of Navarre's wedding and ended up being massacred. Fourteen thousand people in a matter of days." I felt tears start in my eyes and wasn't embarrassed. "All by the sword, and for being Protestant instead of Catholic. I was bawling my head off. A policeman asked me if I needed help!" I shook my head with a chagrined laugh. "I've considered doing a biography of

Catherine de' Medici, but I don't like her. I mean I understand how the Inquisition was necessary to Isabella's faith. Religion played a large part in her decisions. It wasn't political expediency to her. But Catherine had all those people massacred to curry favor with the pope and get even with her son. She does prove that absolute power corrupts absolutely. Even women."

"Oh that one, she's an enigma," Nara said. I could see the gleam of my passion for the past in her eyes as we talked.

I happily shared my feelings on seeing the effigy of Eleanor at Fontevrault during my summer trip, and she eagerly offered me photographs she'd taken of the portal jamb figure reputed to be Eleanor at Chartres Cathedral. Before I knew it an hour had passed and neither of us had had a chance to mingle. Nara gave me her business card and wrote her home number on the back, and we made an eager date to have lunch the following week. Just as I was pocketing Nara's card, I became aware of someone standing just behind me, quietly waiting for my attention.

Sydney gave me a sparkling smile and said, "I knew it was you. How do you know Liz?"

A little flustered, I explained about the radio interview. "You must be what she meant by notable women," I said and hoped she didn't think it was inane.

"Maybe," Sydney said. "Liz knows everybody, though." Sydney quickly pointed out three other politicos, a local actress who had recently signed for a network sitcom, and a coloratura with the Chicago Opera. "And then there's you — Faith Fitzgerald, writer. When Eric introduced you, I didn't recognize your name. But later that night I started wondering if you were the woman who wrote *Isabella*, so I dug it out and there you were on the back. I loved that book."

"Why thank you," I said, touched. Sydney's expression was so open I knew she wasn't idly flattering me. I opened my mouth to say more, then lost what I meant to say. Her eyes were a velvety brown with hints of purple. Not at all like Eric's. I drew breath in again, lost the thought, and would have blushed if Liz hadn't bustled up to us at that moment.

"Where do you know each other from?" Liz looked quite curious. She raised her eyebrows inquiringly at Sydney.

Sydney half-closed her eyes as if answering no to a question Liz hadn't asked. "Faith is a friend of Eric's."

"Oh," Liz said blankly. Then more brightly and to Sydney, "You'll never guess who's back in town."

"Who?" Sydney sipped her drink.

Liz inclined her head toward the doorway. They both looked that direction, and I thanked God they weren't looking at me.

"Heavens," Sydney said. "Does Jan know?"

"I'm not going to tell her," Liz said. "I spent enough time with a wet shoulder."

I managed to smile at Sydney when she glanced back at me. I didn't want her of all people to think anything was wrong. Out of the corner of my eye I could see Renee approaching us. If ever I felt that God had time to worry about my little life, this moment was retribution for all my sins.

"Sydney," Renee said effusively, not even giving

me a glance. "I didn't get a chance the other night to congratulate you on the Roebuck Award."

"Thank you. I didn't know you were there," Sydney said. I saw then her public smile: polite, interested, yet distant.

Liz's hand was under my elbow and she turned me away so that I wasn't in the conversational sphere that included Renee and Sydney. To my profound relief, she steered me gradually to another circle, then whispered in my ear, "Someone you don't need to meet. She's not what I would call a nice person. Lord knows who she's here with. I didn't invite her."

I nodded and said nothing. I had had a moment of pique when I realized that Renee didn't recognize me, but it had quickly passed. Liz's obvious dislike of Renee endeared her further to me. I wished that I hadn't had to leave Sydney that way, but the last thing I wanted was for Renee to see me and say anything that might make Sydney realize that Renee and I had been . . . lovers. No, we were never lovers. We had sex. Or rather, Renee had sex with me; it had not been a shared act except that she had found ways to make me tell her that I wanted what she wanted to do to me. And I *had* wanted it, my body reminded me.

Liz dropped me off in a cluster of fellow academics in the kitchen, but the party had lost its fun for me, and I was sure I didn't want to come face-to-face with Renee. But leaving without a final word with Sydney would be rude, especially since I would be seeing her again on Sunday. I glanced surreptitiously into the living room and saw Renee going into the den. Sydney was warming her hands in front of the fire with a pensive frown that melted away when she saw me in the reflection of the mirror over the mantel.

As I crossed the room I was aware that her velvet brown gaze never left me. I answered her smile in the reflection with one of my own. It wasn't until I was abreast of her that she turned and I looked into her eyes instead of the reflection.

The reflection had shielded me from the warm greeting in her eyes, and for a moment I was dizzy. She looked at me for a long moment before mercifully releasing me from her stare by looking down into the fire.

I found my breath. "I need to be going, but I'm glad I ran into you. Can I bring anything on Sunday?"

"Nothing at all. I love to cook — it's how I relax. When you talk to Eric, tell him I've perfected my lasagna. You *can* bring a very large appetite." She glanced up and I could see the hot, dancing orange of the fire shimmering across her face.

"I will," I managed. I smiled a good-bye and went to find Liz.

"Don't say you're leaving," she said after I thanked her for inviting me.

"I really have to. But I've enjoyed myself," I said. "When I'm settled in my new apartment, I'll return the invitation."

She saw me to the door and cheerily waved good-bye. I was at the bottom of the last flight of stairs, when someone above called my name.

My hand was on the knob. All I had to do was turn it and run. But a fragment of self-respect asserted itself, and I waited for Renee to catch up to me for what now seemed an inevitable meeting. Maybe this was something I just had to do.

"I knew it was you," she said, just as Sydney had.

Her mouth was too wide for her face. It was the first thing I thought when I saw her, and in spite of myself I remembered that mouth on me.

"Same old Faith," she said, with a light laugh. "Am I going to have to make you answer me?"

It was so lightly said I should not have reacted to it, but I did. "You can't make me do anything anymore, Renee."

Her smile stilled and she stared at me, clearly intrigued. It was as if no time had passed at all and she only wanted me because I tried to resist. "Really?"

She wasn't beautiful, but her manner and bearing were compelling. I had seen people stare at her — perhaps it was her five-eleven height and slender figure. Her thick, honey-blonde hair fell attractively into her gray-blue eyes. Those eyes were as wild as I remembered them, lit just now with intent as she fixed her gaze on my lips.

I said coldly, leaning away, "I'm not interested."

Renee crowded a little closer to me. She wore the same scent she had worn all those years ago, and it was still intoxicating. "At least tell me what you're up to these days. I think about you from time to time."

I bet you do. "I don't have time at the moment," I said as I went out the door, leaving her standing there.

I realized then that I should have called a cab before I left Liz's, but there was a small motel about a block west and I'd be able to call from there. To my dismay, Renee caught up to me again.

"Need a lift?"

"No, thank you."

"Where are you living these days?"

I increased my pace and didn't answer.

"I might think you were running away from me," Renee said. "I don't bite."

"No, I don't suppose you do. But I don't want to pursue an acquaintance with you. There's no point to it."

"An acquaintance? We've done too much to be merely acquaintances," Renee said. She kept pace with me and after a minute said, "You've gone back to men, haven't you?"

I was so surprised I stumbled a little.

Renee's tone was smug. "None of my business, I suppose. I just never would have thought you would. You loved what we did. I remember what it was like with you. In some ways there's never been anyone like you since."

The night had turned cold. I shivered and wrapped my arms around myself. "I never loved it," I snapped, knowing I lied.

The chilled air rang with Renee's mocking laugh. "No, not when you begged for it. Certainly not when you —"

"Stop it," I said insistently. "I've gone on with my life. I like my life now. I don't need you in it. I don't need you making trouble for me."

"Trouble," she echoed. In the wan streetlight, her blonde curls were washed with silver. She put her hand on my arm. "Faith . . ."

I yanked myself away from her. "Don't." In spite of myself, I stopped and turned to her. "Look, my memories are not pleasant ones. I don't want to have even an acquaintance with you. I don't see the point."

"You're afraid I'll tell someone about us, aren't you? I remember how insistent you were on silence before."

I didn't like her having any power over me. I saw a predatory look cross her face, then she leaned toward me. "Of course you weren't silent all the time. Do you remember?" Her voice was low. I had forgotten how it cut through me. No matter how much I tried to stop my ears, I heard every word. "Do you remember how loud you were the first time? And that time in the science lab? Do you remember all the things you would say when I finally got you into bed? What about the time outside Swift Hall? That was incredible. You said fu —"

"Stop it!" No, I vowed. I won't go through this again. I am not a virginal schoolgirl caught up in her body's first passions.

"Maybe you don't want me," Renee said. "But I'll never believe you've given up on women. So right now you're with a man. You'll come back eventually."

"Not to you," I said. Then I realized what I'd admitted.

She smiled and without warning cupped my face. I pulled away, stunned that she would touch me when I'd made it so plain I didn't want her to.

I was too stunned. She saw it. And I knew it. Her hands had been soft against my cheeks. But Eric's hands are soft, too, my mind cried. But not the same. My body was electrified, and telling it that

62

these feelings were an abomination, a sin, made no impression.

I was shuddering as I said, "Damn you, Renee. Don't do this to me."

"Do what? This?" Before I could back away, even if I had wanted to, her hands were on my waist, then over my ribs, and she cupped my breasts.

I felt the ground turn to water under me. My vision narrowed to only her face as her touch ignited me. Time stretched as she tipped her head down to mine. I remembered what it felt like to anticipate her kiss. How she would move so slowly toward me. How I would long to close the distance and finally ask her to kiss me.

She whispered in my ear, "You can't fight your nature, Faith."

"I can," I said, before I realized I had admitted a second time that my nature was . . . that I was . . . like her.

My senses were spinning, but I found one moment of clarity. I might want women, but I did not want Renee Callahan. My skin chilled and I pushed her away. "I don't want you," I said coolly. "Please don't touch me again."

"Suit yourself." She turned away. "Sure you don't want a lift? No? Well, good-bye, then." She walked a few steps towards Liz's, then turned back. Her eyes took on a feral glint. "Faith, I won't make trouble for you. I care enough to wish you would accept the truth, though."

I turned and walked away with my dignity in tatters.

* * * * *

I got home late enough to go straight to my room without running into Michael or my parents. I wanted to scrub myself in the shower again, but I slipped into a nightgown and into bed, huddling not so much for warmth, but for the comfort that comes with being warm in your own bed.

Comfort didn't come. I was beset with unwanted memories. I told myself that Renee was wrong. She had spoken nothing but lies. Everything was wrong. I didn't have the feelings Renee had aroused in me. The feelings were lies.

We had not left a late lecture and wandered through the building looking for any unlocked room. We had not stumbled inside the science lab. She had not sat on one of the tables, leaning back on her hands, legs open and ready to wrap around me. I had not seized her hips so hard I left scratches, I had not buried my face into her wetness. I had not been drunk on the taste of her.

I had not, lying on my back, begged her to straddle me and bring herself to me again so I could feel the slick wet of her on my lips again. I had not been thirsty for her until, for once, she pushed me away.

It had not happened. It was a lie. It couldn't be real.

Because if it was real, then Renee was right. I wanted to be with women and I was damned.

"Merciful Mary," I whispered. I rarely looked to the Christ figure in church, but always to the sweet and gentle Queen of Heaven when I was troubled.

I stumbled for the old words and sought their familiar comfort. "Hail Mary, full of grace . . ." But even her comfort eluded me.

4

A woman clothed with the sun, and the moon under her feet, and upon her head a crown of twelve stars.

— REVELATION 12:1

I wouldn't say I was hiding myself when I stayed in my room most of Saturday and read research material I'd downloaded. I didn't cower under the covers, but I avoided my parents and strategically went down for my meals when I knew they were both gone. I didn't need another confrontation with them. Between my parents and Renee, I felt hollow and limp.

But not cowed. If they were going to slam the door behind me, then let them. And I had told Renee — the symbol of all the feelings I didn't want to acknowledge — to go away again. Without Renee to remind me, the feelings would go away as well. If I just concentrated on something else for a while. Like my book, or my new apartment.

James would never know how much his advice affected my life. There was no way I could tell him. Our friendship was not the type where he would appreciate either my gratitude or the responsibility for having had such an influence. Besides, only time would tell if I should be grateful to him.

When I could clear my mind enough to work, I went through the articles about Eleanor I'd downloaded from the Medieval Academy of America. Much of the materials concerned her Court of Love where the rules of courtly love in all their complicated manners were explained.

Rule: A Knight may love a Lady who is married, but may not love an unmarried Lady unless he is of sufficient station to ask for her hand.

Rule: If a Knight loves a Lady who is married, he may hide in his shield some remembrance of her, but no one else may know.

Rule: If a Knight loves a Lady who is married, he may, under certain conditions, woo the Lady to a display of returned love, but no others shall ever know of it.

The conditions to allow adultery were numerous, complicated, and mostly concerned for the Lady's reputation and her needs. For example, a young Lady with an elderly husband might be excused a lapse in her marriage vows if the Knight is particularly persistent, persuasive, and properly humble.

They were worse than the Balk Rule in baseball. I laughed when I read the other conditions, some of which seemed arbitrary, impossible to achieve or tacked on later to get rid of a loophole in an earlier rule. Eleanor's Court of Love were having fine sport with their idle time, in between petty bickerings, blood feuds, and schemings by the various knights (when not in the Holy Land on crusade) to get their hands on someone else's land.

I had to wade through considerable material on the Court of Love to discern aspects of her personality. Most of her biographies, particularly the shorter synopses of her achievements, dwell on the Court of Love as Eleanor's primary accomplishment. This makes her seem foolish and occupied with feminine affairs of the heart. They use the Court of Love to balance out a lifetime of political astuteness, a biting wit, and an ability to take action, ignoring the fact that in addition to affairs of the heart, the Court of Love set out the rules of conduct for the upper class, praised learning and encouraged literacy. It elevated bards to protected status and charged all knights with the protection of the weak. Eleanor's notions of noble behavior would forever influence the French and English consciousness.

In the early evening my mother called me to the phone, her tone and expression laden with disapproval. I didn't feel at all guilty about not mentioning Meg's impending arrival. It was Eric, calling to remind me he was picking me up tomorrow afternoon to go to Sydney's.

"Sydney says that she has perfected her lasagna," I told him.

"She did? When did you see her?"

"At a party last night. The woman who did the radio interview invited me and 'other notables' as she put it. Sydney was one."

Eric chuckled. "She's that, all right. I'm glad you got a chance to talk. Sweetie, I have to run, but I'll pick you up at five-thirty, okay?"

I agreed and hung up before I realized I should have told him I was moving next week. He would be surprised and no doubt want to know why. My explanation would be, of course, that I was both old enough and independent enough to warrant privacy and my own household, and my younger sister's return with an infant made it practical. He might not understand the suddenness of my decision, and I could hardly mention how seeing Renee had thrown me into an inner turmoil I thought long defeated. But I knew he would be supportive. It was one of the reasons I was fond of him.

"I said I was offline tonight, and I meant it." Sydney paused with her hands over the lasagna dish. There was a smear of ricotta on the phone where she'd pushed the speaker option to answer it.

"But Syd, we have to have a response to them in the morning." John had never known how to take no for an answer. That's why he worked for her.

"Morning ends at eleven fifty-nine. It'll be first on the list before staff meeting, okay? Leave a voice mail for Cheryl to that effect. I really need an evening off.

My brother's coming over. And his . . . friend." Was that the right word for Faith? Eric had never shown this much interest in a woman before, not that Sydney knew about anyway. But they didn't seem like lovers.

"Maybe you could call me back after they leave."

Sydney counted to ten, then said, "I'm going to sleep after they leave. Sleep, John. It's a thing many people do. I thought I'd give it a try tonight."

John didn't laugh. He was oblivious to all forms of humor and sarcasm. "Well, don't blame me if we don't get our comments in on time. McClarren's notorious for closing the comment period early."

"Okay, I won't blame you. When have I ever blamed you for anything?"

John piffed into the phone. "I'm hanging up now, *pija.*"

"I know what that means, *pito*." The phone clattered.

She finished layering the pasta over her carefully nurtured sausage and olives. She found herself thinking about the housing policy John wanted comments on and took herself to task.

"I wanted a night off, so I'd better make the most of it."

Duchess opened one yellow eye from her sleeping perch in the sunny kitchen bay window. She closed it again without moving a whisker.

"So I'm boring you?"

Duchess didn't respond in any way, not even a flick of her tail. Sydney turned her mind to Eric and how long it had been since she'd really talked to him. They let too much time go by. Of course they couldn't just talk about family stuff with Faith there.

Faith. Still waters ran deep, Sydney suspected. She remembered looking at Faith's eyes in the mirror. Green eyes, with blue in their depths. The waters were very still, but they shimmered.

When I saw Sydney's home, I was struck by the difference between the choices brother and sister had made. Sydney's home occupied the top floor of one of the regal, old Stone Street condominium mid-rises that lined the curve of Lake Michigan just north of the downtown Chicago Loop. It was only about a half mile from my new apartment but in a completely different income bracket. Eric lived in a lovely Evanston split-level with two acres out back for his beloved Irish setters, an enclosed heated pool and spa, and enough rolling yard to stage a soccer game for an army of children. Sydney could have gone another mile north and escaped the bustle of the downtown district, but she was as close to the heart of the city as she could get, and in a building that wasn't high enough to completely escape the noise of the city streets fifteen floors below.

It was high enough for a heart-stopping view of the upper Miracle Mile and the vast blackness of Lake Michigan. Lights bobbed on the water as pleasure craft and shipping tankers shared the fading daylight.

Absorbed in the view though I was, I didn't miss the affectionate bear hug Eric gave Sydney, followed by a frank appraisal. "You work too hard," Eric pronounced. "But you don't look as scary as you did at that dinner."

"Scary?" Sydney turned to me. "Did I look scary?"

"Not at all," I said. "I have no idea what he means."

"Sure you do," Eric said. "She looked so official and politician-like I wondered what happened to the sister who put my best running shoes in Mom's composter."

"Eric! Stop it," Sydney said, playfully slapping him as she took his coat. "What will Faith think?"

"That you're my favorite sister."

"I'm your *only* sister," Sydney retorted. She took my coat and hung it in the foyer closet with Eric's. "Come into the sitting room. I've got a fire going. Think about what you'd like to drink. Nonalcoholic, that is." She threw me an apologetic glance.

"Fine by me," I said, as I tore my gaze from the Tiffany glass skylight in the foyer ceiling. "I never acquired the taste. Not even Communion wine."

"I liked it too much," Sydney said, looking at me seriously for a moment. She glanced up at her brother, then smiled. "Glenfiddich, not Communion wine. Eight years, ten months, and twenty-one days, in case you were wondering."

"I wasn't," Eric said. "But thanks for sharing."

"Don't let his nonchalance fool you," Sydney said to me as she led the way across the large and spacious living room. "I owe my sobriety to him. And a good therapist."

I digested this information as we walked through the living room. I had developed the impression that Eric's sister could be single-minded in her pursuit of what she wanted and that she succeeded by strength and perseverance. Finding out she had had a drinking problem proved Sydney was human.

Compared with Eric's deep mahoganies and nubby tweeds, Sydney's home was cool with white carpets and vivid fabrics splashed brilliant reds, blues, and greens. Borders of Tiffany-style stained glass framed the windows, in keeping with the building's art deco exterior. The fireplace was framed with elegant marble fluting right out of the Roaring Twenties. What both homes had in common was simple elegance that didn't look nearly so expensive as it must be. The Van Allen family had a lot of money, old and new.

My impression of cool aloofness faded when I saw the sitting room. A third of the room was dominated by an old desk, computer workstation, and office gadgets, including a fax machine. The desk was worn and grooved with the scars of many years of work.

I fell in love with the rest of the room — a large fireplace threw an ocean of heat into the comfortable chairs and sofas in crushed velvets and soft weaves. Instead of the hard, clean jewel tones of the living room, everything in this inner sanctum was softer, warmer, and gentler. The pristine white carpet gave way to a dove gray Berber. A low lavender footstool appeared to be covered by a fluffy gray rug until I realized the rug was peering at me suspiciously. The cat closed its eyes once it had consigned me to the ranks of the uninteresting. I sank into an enormous chair in muted lavender and sea green, surrounded by soft pillows. I immediately wanted to put my head down and burrow deeper with an old, beloved book.

"Be careful of that chair," Sydney said. "It puts people to sleep."

I struggled upright. "I think it's bewitched," I said. "It made me want to read *Ivanhoe* and eat apples."

Sydney laughed. *"Little Women,* right?"

I grinned. "That's amazing."

"Sydney can identify almost any quote," Eric said, settling into a sofa corner. He stretched out his long legs.

Sydney's back was to us as she dropped ice cubes into glasses. "What would you like? I squeezed juice this morning."

"What kind of juice," Eric asked suspiciously.

"Strawberry-kiwi-lime with apple and grapes." Sydney laughed at the expression on Eric's face. "Okay, I cleaned out the fridge."

"I'll have juice," I said. "It sounds great."

"You're a wonderful guest," Sydney said, handing me a glass. "Actually, it's good. Here," she said to Eric. "You get sparkling water."

I sipped the juice. "I can feel the vitamins already."

"It has that effect on me, too." Sydney poured herself a glass and then settled gracefully in front of the fire on a large square pillow covered with petit point.

"I bet Faith could stump you," Eric said.

"Oh stop." Sydney pursed her lips at Eric and turned to me. "He's been trying to stump me on a quote for years. Other people do it all the time, but he's never managed," she said, with a wicked glance at him. Eric stuck his tongue out at her.

"You must have an incredible memory," I said. I wondered why I had ever thought her cold.

Her smile turned serious. "I think that alcohol reformatted my hard drive," she said, tapping her forehead. "I was unfit to practice even the most basic law for about two years and spent all my time reading. And reading. And reading. It was how I got back to reality."

"Reality leaves a lot to the imagination," I said.

Sydney opened her mouth, and I could almost see the cerebral computer disks spinning. After a few moments, she said, "John Lennon."

We smiled at each other, and I realized anew that her eyes were brown, but velvet where Eric's were crystal. She looked away, leaving me with an odd sensation in the pit of my stomach.

Both Eric and Sydney were too polite to talk about topics I knew nothing about, but it was unavoidable. A failing elderly aunt was news to Eric, and Sydney hadn't yet heard about the birth of a second cousin.

"Sorry, Faith," Eric said. "It must be boring."

I shook my head. "No, really. But I must confess that I can't keep your family tree straight in my head."

Sydney chuckled. "My grandmother, that's my father's mother, was married and widowed three times and had two children each marriage. My father was child number three and son number one. He has one brother, three half-sisters and a half-brother. All of them except my father have been married at least twice with kids from each marriage. I have trouble keeping it clear, and I've had years of practice. It makes our family holidays very, very large."

Eric snorted. "As we are all going to experience this year. Mom wants to do the big holiday. She put out the word to the aunts and uncles about four months ago, and it looks like with a few exceptions everyone is going to come. She's guessing about a hundred adults and sixty-five kids for dinner."

"Wow," I said, before I could help myself. "I wouldn't want to be the one who brings the potato salad."

They both burst out laughing, Sydney falling back on the pillow. All at once I realized how lovely the rest of her was. Her features were too pronounced to be pretty, but striking in combination. Her cashmere sweater outlined a lean figure, and I glanced down at my hands, thinking that her breasts would fill them.

My heart stopped. For about five seconds I couldn't breathe. Sydney's laughter died and she wiped her eyes, then turned her head to look at me. I could breathe again. I wanted to breathe her in.

Her eyes widened. "We're not laughing at you," she said, rising up onto one elbow. "You hit the nail on the head, that's all."

The firelight was dancing on her throat and mouth the way it had the night of Liz's party.

Eric nudged me gently. "Are you okay, sweetie?"

"I'm sorry," I managed to say. "I was floored by the idea of anyone being able to entertain that many people outside of a hotel in this day and age." I met women all the time. Until now only Renee had affected me this way. My pulse was hammering in my throat.

Eric smiled fondly. "That's our mom. She says once a decade you need to air out the grand ballroom to fight the mildew."

"She sounds like a practical woman," I said, feeling very far away. I've always liked looking at women. The way they are always busy, how they move their hands and walk. Their faces please my eyes. But only Renee had ever made my skin burn. Until now.

"She is," Sydney was saying. "The gardens are just a means of using up the manure from the stables. And so on." She looked at me a little oddly, and I summoned up a smile.

"There's nothing quite so astonishing as common sense," I said.

"Emerson," Sydney said. "Let's have dinner."

The food was so good that I managed to regain my composure. Sydney hadn't been idly boasting about her lasagna — the sauce was rich and smooth with olives and plum tomatoes. Garlic toast with goat cheese and freshly chopped chives accompanied it, followed by what Sydney called her great vice: chocolate mousse in chocolate bowls topped with chocolate sauce.

"This is rather chocolate overkill, don't you think? You could have done a raspberry sauce, you know," Eric said. One of the things I liked about him was that he enjoyed food. Sydney obviously did, too.

Sydney sniffed. "I don't understand the tendency to ruin perfectly good chocolate with fruit."

"I'm with you," I said, making a face at Eric. "There's no such thing as chocolate overkill. However, I have developed a taste for Godiva chocolate-covered orange peels. On special occasions, and then I have to go to confession."

Sydney's shudder turned into a smile. "Well, *ego te absolvo*. To each her own." She glanced at her brother. "What are you smiling about, Eric?"

"I was just thinking how glad I am you like each other. I thought you would, and I didn't want to be wrong."

I did like Sydney. I liked her very much. I'd be

much happier if I weren't fighting other, inappropriate feelings. I glanced at her, she smiled, and time stood still. It couldn't have, not really. The feeling was absurd.

Sydney abruptly looked away, saying, "Let's have coffee in front of the fire."

"I'll help you clear up," I offered.

"No need, the dishes just go in the sink. One of the joys of being the idle rich is Lucy, who stops in for a few hours every day to clean up, take my dry cleaning in, buy groceries, and be generally indispensable."

"Idle rich," Eric scoffed. "You're hardly idle, Syd. Neither am I."

I could tell that the idea of being thought "idle rich" bothered him. I admired him for working as hard as he did when he could have been a playboy. No doubt his family money had allowed him to buy his architectural firm, but it wasn't a hobby. He didn't dabble at architecture any more than Sydney dabbled at law.

Despite Sydney's protests, I helped carry our dishes into the kitchen while Sydney made cappuccino. I was already in love with the sitting room, and I lost my heart again to the old-fashioned but functional kitchen. It was larger than my entire apartment. The iron stove had claw feet, but the eight burners obviously worked. There were two Sub-Zero refrigerators and a deep freeze. There was a large oven big enough for a fifty-pound turkey and a smaller one for projects not quite so vast. Microwave and convection ovens were also built into the cabinetry. I asked her about the tile, which looked very old and Italian, and she described the various restoration projects she'd undertaken since buying the condominium about six years earlier. Her desire to keep the interiors faithful to their original nineteen-twenty appearance hadn't stopped her from adding all the modern conveniences, but appliances like the dishwasher were hidden behind oak cabinets with aged porcelain insets.

We settled into our earlier chairs with fragrant cappuccinos.

"May I ask you both a question?"

Eric nodded at me and Sydney said, "Fire away."

"What's it like being from such a remarkable family? Not just wealthy, but . . . vivid. At Christmas a lot of fame and personality will be gathered under one roof."

Eric sat up a little, while Sydney turned her head to look into the fire. I saw her bite her lower lip.

"It is challenging," Eric said. "We're lucky in our parents. They like steadiness. They've been married for forty years and don't see how special they are. Mom's matter-of-fact about everything, and Dad thinks everything we do is fine by him." He shot a glance at Sydney. "Well, almost everything we do. I never worried about measuring up to the rest of the family. Mom and Dad are what matter."

"It was easier for you. I'm not sure why," Sydney said, looking across the room at her brother. "Maybe I felt it because my drummer really has a different beat. If I was going to go against the grain, I wanted to do it spectacularly. And that just got me into trouble with alcohol, and relationships. It took me a long time to see how I fit into our family, and how . . ." She searched for words. "Knowing that I did fit brought me back to sanity."

"You weren't that far gone," Eric said.

"Don't bet on it," Sydney retorted. She turned to me. "Are you close to your brother?"

"Close. Hmm." I thought about all the things Michael didn't know about me, that I didn't know about him, and I still vividly remembered his intercession during my father's violent outburst. "We do care about each other and feel protective. I didn't know how much he meant to me until he had an accident. In the Navy. He was in an engine-room fire and had burns on thirty percent of his body, across the chest, arms and back. He suffered . . ." I broke off to clear my throat. "He was in a lot of pain. Still is. At first he took some sort of painkiller that kept him from dreaming, well at least that he could recall. I think I dreamed his dreams for him — I had nightmares about fire for almost a month after it happened. But are we close? We don't share a lot of the day to day, but the connection's there. It's certainly stronger than the one I feel with my sister."

Sydney was watching me intently, and I knew she hadn't missed the misting of tears in my eyes as I remembered Michael's painful struggle. I didn't usually talk about such things.

"Eric dragged me to an AA meeting. He may say now that I wasn't that far gone, but I was a person I don't ever want to be again. He sat next to me night after night while I fumed about him playing the big brother, and little by little the message of the meetings began to sink in. I have my reservations about some of the AA dogma, but there is magic working at those meetings. He didn't stop coming with me until I got up, introduced myself, and admitted I was an alcoholic."

Eric shifted uncomfortably. "You'd have done the same for me."

"I'd never need to. And that's the difference between us."

"I know," he said. "I'm stuffy and boring."

"You're not," I protested. "Stuffy and boring people do not put Thai peanut sauce on their ice cream."

"Eeeww," Sydney said. "That's disgusting."

"It's good," Eric muttered, but he was smiling.

Sydney wrinkled her nose at him and turned to me. "My turn. I told you about fitting in my family. How do you fit in yours, Faith?"

"Well, I'm . . ." I paused with my mouth open and searched for words. A writer's trick is to picture a scene and then describe it. I pictured a Thanksgiving from my teens and saw us gathered: my mother's father the tailor; my mother the mainstay of the Altar Society; my brother the Naval officer; my sister the baby of the family; my father the assistant postmaster; his father the overwhelmed alcoholic Irishman who married one of the strong Walescu sisters, creating the Fitzgerald branch; his wife, my grandmother the beautiful and utterly cold matriarch; her brother the monsignor. But I couldn't see myself. I looked again — my mother the martyr, my brother the angry, my sister the flirt, my father the sanctimonious. Where did I fit?

Where was the scholar, the writer, the woman who found joy in the past, who taught with such happiness? Why did my mind turn to teen years, when self-identity is so fragile and unformed? Before Renee showed me how to hate myself? Long before I became someone I could admire?

"Faith?" Eric leaned forward and touched my knee. "Where did you go?"

I fought down a blush and glanced from him to Sydney, who had gotten up from her pillow to add more chocolate sprinkles to her cappuccino. My throat began to ache and I knew that if I blinked they would see the tears I didn't want to acknowledge. "Sorry," I mumbled. I sipped my cappuccino and made myself breathe deeply. "I didn't think that would be a difficult question for me to answer."

Eric put his arm around me and said, "You don't have to answer."

"Certainly not," Sydney said, sitting down on the arm of my chair. "I'm sorry I asked."

"Don't be." I pushed myself gently away from Eric, feeling steadied by his undemanding physical support. "You hit a nerve I didn't know I had. I don't think — I don't think I fit in my family."

"Why not?" Sydney looked into my eyes without flinching. "Are you so different?"

"I couldn't tell you if it's me or them." A lie. I was the different one. The unnatural one. "I've been meaning to tell you, Eric, that I've gotten my own apartment."

Eric gave me an intent look, then his gaze seemed to turn inward.

"You live at home," Sydney said, not really a question.

"I'm a good Catholic daughter," I said. "At least I was."

Eric patted my knee again and settled back into

the sofa. I had felt warm and comforted while he held me. His arms were a safe place. Sydney still sat on the arm of my chair, making my nerves prickle. I looked up at her, and I knew she was dangerous.

"You still are," she said, gazing down at me. "You owe it to your parents to use the life they gave you. To not do what your heart calls you to do holds them in contempt. It holds God in contempt."

I swallowed painfully, then managed a weak smile. "You'd be dynamic in a pulpit."

She didn't answer or move for a moment, then pushed her hair back in a nervous gesture. "It's the politician in me," she said. "Politics is part preaching and part peddling." She stood up and stretched. "How'd we get so maudlin?"

"Faith started it," Eric said. "It's the historian in her. Piercing questions and always looking for cause and effect."

"Feel like a game of pool?" Sydney asked. "I never get to play these days." It took all my strength of will not to watch her cross the room.

Eric looked at me and I nodded, eager to have their attention away from me. I tried hard to act as naturally as possible, but inside I was trembling and only a few heartbeats away from panic.

The game room was off a wide hallway that divided the rear half of the floor in half again. Sydney waved to the left. "Guest suite is the first door. The master suite is back there. And behind that door is a great deal of exercise equipment I don't have time to use. I haven't found a use for these rooms on the right, but I put the pool table back in this corner for the view."

What a view it was. We were looking away from

the lake. To the west the sprawl of Chicago glittered unbroken as far as the horizon. To the southwest was downtown Chicago with most of the buildings dwarfed by the final looming presence of the Sears Tower. Closer to us the Water Tower and Hancock Center twinkled, and the Eisenhower Expressway, never empty, gleamed with headlights.

Then Sydney switched the lights on in the room and I caught my breath. She looked at me with a pleased smile.

"She did a nice job, didn't she?" Eric sounded proud.

"I'm . . . agog." I said. "It looks like Rick's Place in *Casablanca.*"

Sydney grinned and Eric applauded. "Thank you for the compliment! Pick a cue," she said.

"I've never played before," I admitted. They both offered to help and racked up a noncompetitive game punctuated with explanations of where Sydney had found the cabana ceiling fans, the old mahogany bar complete with brass footrests, and the white baby grand piano. Eric had helped with the structural modifications necessary to support the weight of the bar and the spa in the master suite.

Inevitably, Eric helped me with my pool shots. Another man might have made something of the opportunities to put his arms around me from behind, positioning my hands just so, helping me sight along the cue, but I never felt flustered by his nearness. Rather I felt the same security I'd felt earlier. It was pleasant, and I accepted the comfort of it. I could go on this way with him. It would be so different than with Renee, but I would be happy. It would be so easy to be happy with him.

Eric excused himself for a few minutes, and Sydney took her next shot. She missed and left me with a not-so-easy opportunity with the 7-ball.

"Are you sure you want to do that? The two is a better possibility."

I looked at the relative positions and said, "Wouldn't I have to bank the shot?" I knew I'd never make it.

"Yes, but the cue position's not difficult. Like this."

Just as Eric had, she came around to my side and put her arms around me from behind. Her arms weren't as long as Eric's, so her body pressed against mine. Her hands wrapped around mine on the cue and then she let go to tip my head. She sighted along the cue, her cheek to mine. When she spoke, her breath swirled around my ear. "That should do it. Smack the cue ball sharply, but not hard."

I drew the cue slowly back, not wanting to end the moment. Why was this feeling of Sydney next to me so different from the feeling of Eric? I felt her breasts against my side and the heat of her breath whispering past my ear, and I wanted more. After what seemed like an eternity of filling my head with the scent of her hair, I gave the cue ball what I hoped was a smack. We held our positions as it flew across the table, ricocheted, and tapped the 2-ball into the side pocket.

"Good shot," Eric said from the doorway.

Sydney stood up slowly saying "But of course" while I resisted the urge to leap guiltily to my feet. Fortunately, Eric came to the table to study his shot and thankfully didn't notice my blushing cheeks.

The rest of the game was uneventful, but the

damage to my self-image was irreparable. I didn't
know who I was anymore, and I felt high. Renee had
liked to smoke pot after sex, and it had left me
blurry and the edges of my memory soft. This high
was sharp and crystal clear. Everything about Sydney
was a bright sparkle, and I memorized the freckle
where her throat met her shoulder. Her left earlobe
had an extra crinkle. When she pushed up her
sweater sleeves, I took note of the light brown down
on her forearms.

We said goodnight with laughter and a promise
from Eric to have Sydney over to dinner as soon as
he got back from his next business trip. It was un-
spoken but understood that Eric's invitation came
from both of us, and I knew that the evening had
significantly moved Eric and me closer together in his
mind.

I had never felt so apart from him as I did when
he drove me home. I felt like a fraud and didn't
know what to do. He saw me to the door and kissed
me lightly on the lips.

"Do you need help moving or anything? I'm sorry
I'll be gone."

"No, I'll be fine. I really don't have that much."

"Leave the phone number with my service as soon
as you get it so I can call you." He looked down at
me with a tenderness that alarmed me. "Will you
miss me while I'm in Hong Kong?"

"Yes," I said honestly. I would.

"Good," he said, giving me another kiss. "Miss me
every day, please."

I pushed him away playfully and watched him get
into his car. It would be so easy to love him. Easier
if I still didn't feel the heat of Sydney's touch.

5

*A time to rend, and a time to sew; a time to keep
silence, and a time to speak.*

— ECCLESIASTES 3:7

Sydney stared at the phone. She hadn't felt this
way in a long time. She should be working, but she
had found herself staring into space again, trying
hard to think about nothing.

Thinking about nothing was better than thinking
about Faith. She'd been struggling with too persistent
memories of Faith all week. Cheryl had noticed her
distraction. Even John, who tended to notice little
unless it pertained to him, had told her to buckle

down. She was almost never distracted, and that's why they noticed.

Thinking about nothing was easier in a bar. It was easy to be alone in a bar, easy to clear your mind and just let the time pass with the help of a smooth single malt. Even though she wanted a drink just about every day, she hadn't wanted to go to a bar in years.

She stared at the phone and knew she should call someone. Alan Stevens would be best. She needed to be reminded of what stood in the balance for her continued good behavior. Mark O'Leary's intimate little dinner had turned out to be her unveiling to party bigwigs as Mark's favored candidate for the next senatorial race. Mark had even gone so far as to make sure everyone knew that he knew she was a lesbian but that with her squeaky-clean personal history since she'd quit the bottle, he thought she would still beat anyone the GOP put up against her, especially since "Syd's promised she'll be good."

Squeaky-clean. How about lusting after your brother's girlfriend, a woman who is probably as virginal as she looks and most likely doesn't know you're a lesbian. Eric would not have mentioned it. He still had trouble coming out as a man with a gay sister.

She'd known since Liz's party that Faith intrigued her. And when Eric had so casually put his arm around Faith — she'd known then she was in trouble. And instead of resisting temptation, she'd used Faith's pool shot to be close to her. Faith had been too pliable to know Sydney was gay. Straight women tended to go rigid when a known lesbian touched them, and Faith hadn't. She had melted into Sydney without any hint of awkwardness. Eric was damned lucky.

He deserved a woman like Faith. Intelligent and witty, attractive without any help from make-up. Genuine. With a heart as warm as topaz, not the cold glitter of diamonds like Eric's last serious girlfriend. He didn't tend to get serious very often, but he was serious about Faith.

She stared at the telephone and thought how easy it would be to put on a jacket and walk down the street to the Dorchester. There was a beautiful bar in the basement where one could be discreetly alone, pouring amber Glenfiddich into a heavy lead crystal glass. It was civilized. No one would know. It would be so easy.

The phone was between her and the door and finally, though it took a great deal of effort, she reached for the phone. She knew the number of her AA sponsor by heart, though she hadn't called her for six months. Her sponsor's partner told Sydney she was at the same health club as always.

As her cab slid past the Dorchester, Sydney wanted to jump out. But the cab was going too fast.

Considering the turmoil the announcement had caused, the day I moved out was quite calm. My mother sat in disapproving silence as I took out my boxes. I knew that when Meg showed up, she'd be glad of the empty room. My father was away at a church meeting, a frequent event since his retirement from the post office. Michael asked a friend to help, and it took only two carloads to move my clothes and books. He and his buddy told me I'd picked a nice place and left me there with a happy wave. I'd told my mother I would be back for Sunday mass, but otherwise my new future yawned ahead of me.

Arranging the furniture took only some of my mental energy, though I wanted it to take it all, and writing cards to acquaintances with my new address and phone number was not absorbing enough either. I couldn't get Sydney out of my head. I thought about her almost nonstop but could only recall Eric with a conscious effort.

What was wrong with me? Eric was everything I could want, and with all my heart and mind I wanted to want him. I yearned for the life he could offer me. It was my treacherous body that itched for Sydney. It was a powerful itch that made me recall every moment I'd spent with her and wonder what it would be like to lie next to her in her bed, kiss the soft skin on her thighs, hear her voice raised in passion.

It was with relief that I left a faculty meeting a little bit early to keep my lunch date on Thursday at Water Tower with Nara Rogier. Lunch stretched into a talkathon that lasted most of the afternoon. She had a photographer's eye for details, and I found her remembered descriptions of Canterbury Cathedral and the Tower of London inspiring. We finally left the restaurant and walked to a British shop she knew of to look at the imported table linens. Normally, I would have gone back to my office, but I was enjoying myself far too much. She wanted new linens for her sister, and I found myself buying a set for myself.

We were leaving the shop when she admitted she was hungry again. I glanced at my watch and realized it was after five. We'd eaten at noon. I acted completely on impulse.

"My place is about fifteen minutes by cab. Could I interest you in salad, bread, and cheese?" My menu suggestion was in deference to Nara's vegetarianism.

Her face lit up. "That sounds perfect. But you must be getting sick of me going on and on about my travels."

"Not in the least, really. It's going to help me finish the chapter on Eleanor's first sight of Britain. You'll be wanting to get rid of me."

Dinner was as much fun as lunch, and we washed up afterward in harmony. By then I had told her all about moving out, my parents' strict Catholic beliefs, Michael's accident, and Meg's return.

We took our coffee into the living room. As I settled on the sofa, I caught Nara staring at me.

"What is it? Do I have spinach in my teeth?"

"No," she said. "It's just that you look like someone I was close to when she was your age."

"Who?"

"An old lover, Diane."

I suppose I must have looked a little stunned. Nara was old enough to be my mother, and I hadn't thought about there being older women who were lesbians. Then I felt really stupid.

"I've shocked you," she said. "I'm sorry, but I thought . . . well, let's just say I'm sorry. It's just that you do look a little bit like her when she was your age. It's your eyes, more than anything."

I felt so stupid that I was at a loss for words.

"Perhaps I should be going," Nara finally said. She put down her coffee, looking disappointed.

"It's not you," I managed to say. "It's me. I don't know what I am anymore," I blurted out. "I mean . . . I do know what I am. I don't want to be that way."

She gazed at me solemnly, then said, "Why ever not?"

I realized that if I told her I thought it was a sin, that I'd burn in hell, that my faith would condemn me, that it was contrary to nature, then I'd be saying all those things about her. Nara wasn't Catholic. She wouldn't understand that every Communion reinforced what I'd been taught. That every liturgy sang redemption for what I'd done with Renee if only I never repeated it. I didn't want her to think I was condemning her when I condemned myself.

But I found myself telling her about Renee. The shame and degradation she'd made me feel. Withholding sex until I agreed to do it her way. And then making me beg her to do it her way. What I wanted was nothing. What I needed was nothing. I was nothing to her and nothing to myself.

It wasn't easy to say some of it. At times I had to stop so I could gain my composure again. It was easier when she sat next to me and took my hand, and gently stroked it without saying anything. I felt her understanding and support, and it helped me finish the entire bitter tale.

When I paused to wipe away an errant tear, she said gently, "Faith, have you ever asked yourself what you would have felt if Renee had been a man who had treated you that way?"

I shook my head. "I . . . no. No, I haven't."

"Think about it. Was it how she treated you or that she was a woman that still upsets you so?"

"That's irrelevant. In addition to fornication, my sin was in lying with another woman."

"Forget the church for a moment." She said it as if it was the simplest thing in the world to do.

"I can't," I said, slowly. "I know there are hypocrisies, I know there are conflicting rules, I know how women are second-class citizens, I know the violence that's been done in Christ's name." I took a deep breath. "I know it all. And it doesn't change what my faith gives me."

"Your faith or the church? Are you sure they're the same?" Nara leaned forward to touch my knee. "Not all churches believe I'm an abomination, you know. There are many different Christian faiths."

I shook my head again. "I know you're trying to help."

"I wish I could give you peace," she said in a whisper. "I like you, Faith. I like you very much. If I'd had a daughter I'd have wanted her to be like you." She pulled me against her shoulder and I rested my head. "I'd have wanted her to know that sex should be an ecstasy and that how it works for you doesn't matter as much as the joy you experience and you give your partner."

I mumbled from her shoulder, "My mother told me that a wife submits to her husband's desires and in return he gives her children." I wanted to ask her how I reconciled what I knew myself to be with the lessons my mother and father, the nuns and priests had drummed into my head. They were truly irreconcilable differences.

Nara laughed in my ear. "I don't think your mother would approve of me."

"My mother doesn't approve of anyone." I sat up. "I should stop trying, but it's an ingrained habit."

"What you should probably do is talk to someone," Nara said. "I have a friend who might be able to help you think this through."

"Thanks, but —"

She went over to my desk. "I'm writing his name and number down right here. You only have to call it if you want to. I won't ask."

"Thanks," I managed.

"I've really got to go," she said. "Can you call a cab?"

We talked about inconsequential things until the cab came. I saw her down to the building door, and she gave me a quick kiss on the cheek.

"Call me for lunch again. I'd really enjoy it," she said.

Before I went to bed, I looked at the note Nara had written, then slipped it into my desk. I knew that she had meant well, but I didn't need therapy, I needed absolution.

"*Gallimaufry*," James said from my office door.

"Hmmm." I tried to looked puzzled. "Let me move this jumble of stuff out of your way. What a hodgepodge my office is."

He glared as he sat down. "Is there a word you don't know?"

I grinned. "I've only done better when we ruled out scientific and medical terms, remember?"

He grunted and then looked around my office with a sigh.

"I've moved, you know. Left the nest."

"Really? Was it something I said?" He looked pleased.

"You know it was. I got my own place, and here's my new phone number." Suddenly, I wanted to tell him more, but after unburdening myself in front of Nara — who must have thought me distinctly odd — I wasn't ready to do a repeat.

He took the little card and then shifted uncomfortably in the chair. "I think I pulled a muscle." He pressed his hand to his side. "This whole part of my body is killing me."

"Maybe you should go to the doctor."

"Now who's giving advice?" He continued to knead his side with a wince. "I suppose I shall just have to get used to having aches and pains. Something you wouldn't understand."

"I'm only five years younger than you, you know."

He sighed. "I'm definitely middle-aged. It's the stage of life when you think you'll feel better tomorrow."

I persisted. "How long has it hurt?"

"A couple of weeks. A month, maybe. I don't know how I could have strained it."

"Carrying too many books, probably." I watched him for a moment. "We pay through the nose for our health insurance, so use it."

"Yes, mother," he snapped. "Oh, I suppose if it's not better by next week, I'll go. Satisfied?"

"Yes," I said primly. "Where's my Dilbert?"

He handed over his *Tribune* in return for my *Times*. "It's performance evaluation time for Dilbert."

"I remain very glad not to be working in corporate America."

"We wouldn't survive a week. They seem to want something called pro-duck-tivi-tee."

I frowned. "I'm stumped. I have no idea what that means."

He chortled in his nefarious way, then got up with another wince. "Maybe I'll go to the doctor this week."

"Maybe you should. Otherwise, people will think you're an algophile."

He left after giving me a particularly fine glare.

My mother called me at my office on Friday to tell me that Meg had come. She seemed truly happy and talked almost nonstop about the baby. I assured her I would come for Mass on Sunday and stay for supper afterward. I was relieved that she was ready to make peace.

In the last two days as I concentrated on my research of Eleanor's life in France, I hadn't thought about Sydney very much, to my heartfelt relief. Work would obviously be my cure, and I threw myself into researching events leading up to Eleanor's decision to leave for England.

Eleanor had had a safe, secure life. She was married to the most admired prince in Europe, and she was the most powerful woman in Christendom. Everyone admired her beauty and wit, and she was considered a shrewd businesswoman in dealing with her lands. King Louis was a monk at heart, and most biographers dwelled on the way Eleanor influenced him. More than one of Louis's advisors felt she had undue influence, ignoring the fact that the Aquitaine was still Eleanor's. That made Eleanor her husband's chiefest and wealthiest vassal, let alone any call she may have had on him because she was his wife. So I didn't see her influence as undue, not in the least.

In 1147, she insisted Louis take her on crusade with him. I was becoming attuned to the way she thought, and could hear her firmly stating that she was not going to sit idly at home counting linens and supervising harvests while the men went off to have their fun. Unfortunately, the result was disastrous. Most biographers put the blame squarely on Eleanor: She dallied in Spain, flirted with Sultans, and so on. Only a few include the information that Louis found travel an appallingly messy and expensive business, and fighting made him ill. When he wanted to call the Crusade off, Eleanor wanted to stay and help defend the castle of one of her uncles. Louis dragged her to Spain with him against her will, and a few weeks after their departure Eleanor's uncle was killed. Adding insult to injury, the king's advisors persuaded Louis to make Eleanor pay the debts they had accumulated on their journey.

Eleanor never forgave Louis. Though they would have another daughter within a year, she was already planning her divorce.

When it became clear that the twenty-seven-year-old Eleanor would win her divorce suit — the clerics of France being eager to get rid of a troublesome and sonless queen — the male nobility of Europe descended on her in a feeding frenzy. It may be that the clerics and Louis's advisors thought that they could wrest the Aquitaine from Eleanor in the divorce. They were not successful, and there was no shortage of men who wanted to be its master. And no doubt they thought they would be Eleanor's master, as well. A single woman again, during her journey home from Paris to Poitiers she eluded two would-be abductors who intended to force a marriage on her, by rape if necessary.

Courtiers of every type — Saracens, even — rode into the Aquitaine. Poets, musicians, and lettered men tried to win her. Men from age twelve to sixty pressed their suit. One of them was Henry Plantagenet.

What was it about Henry that made her choose him? The decision was all hers. He was barely eighteen when they married and not yet king of England — and even that wasn't assured. The crown his mother, Maud, had fought for might go to her son, but there was no guarantee. Henry's legacy was no more than potential when Eleanor agreed to the marriage.

After reading all the material I had, with more to come, I thought I had found my angle. Maybe she chose Henry because she couldn't change the world through Louis, nor do it by herself. She needed a man as strong and as ambitious as she was by her side. And Henry really wanted to change the world, not keep it as it was. For Henry, changing the world meant a minor French duke, himself, becoming duke of nearly half of France and then king of all of Britain. It would make him the chiefest prince in Europe, surpassing the hated Louis and his family (who had not supported Maud's claim to Britain) and rivaling the pope himself. If she could help Henry achieve his ambitions, she would be the queen of something she had helped build: the Angevin Empire.

Forget the paneled rooms and fine silks of France. Forget having all of Europe at her feet. She would experience the danger of securing a throne if Henry did succeed Stephen. She knew she would be vilified in France if she married Henry. Out of the wild times that would surely follow their marriage, she could create order. So she turned her back on her civilized Aquitaine and sailed for the wilds of England.

I was writing furiously and not sleeping much, but I still presented myself at my parents' in time to leave for Mass on Sunday. I was astonished that my mother kissed me; I hadn't seen her looking this happy in years.

"David is just the smartest little boy. Come look," she said.

My father gave me only passing notice, being engrossed in dangling a bear in front of the chubby toddler. Meg's greeting was exuberant, and even Michael had more smiles than grimaces. All in all, I felt like I'd walked onto the set of *The Waltons,* and I didn't have any speaking lines. I played with David a little, but having never had any maternal urges I let my mother supplant me after a few minutes.

In a flurry we all piled into the enormous Lincoln Town Car that was my father's pride and joy. We were always early because my father liked to arrive before the other ushers. I saw my mother to the family pew and then walked up the long aisles to admire the stained glass from the back of the cathedral. I always did it, and I badly needed something to feel unchanged to me.

St. Anthony's congregation numbered over three thousand, making it the third largest church in Chicagoland. Without exception the ten o'clock Sunday Mass was standing room only. Its size warranted a head usher, my father, who supervised fifteen other men who took turns as ushers.

Meg and my mother were gathering a steady flow of congratulations on David's winsome manners and Meg's return to Chicago. I looked my fill at the brilliant hues in the stained glass, then decided I'd wait in the foyer for a while. Meg and Mom were talking a language I didn't understand, and I was better off on the edge.

I looked over the bulletin board to pass the time. I wanted a television and a bicycle, and there was a chance someone would be selling one or the other. While I searched, a young man in a clerical collar came into the church by the street door, tacked a paper to the board, and went out the street door again, rather than back toward the sacristy. Not a St. Anthony's priest, obviously, since he was wearing jeans. All of this was odd enough to make me curious about what he posted.

It was a vivid pink flyer that read, "DIGNITY is about being cherished by our church as much as we cherish it. Gay men, lesbians, bisexuals and transsexuals, or any other person who needs support are welcome at our weekly meetings." An address and a twenty-four-hour hotline number were at the bottom.

In a daze, I read the flyer again. How could this group exist? Did they ignore the passages of the Bible that plainly condemned homosexuality? A support group could not rewrite the Bible.

I took the flyer off the board, knowing it would be removed as soon as one of the priests saw it. There had been something automatic about the way the priest had put it up, as if he did it every week. If so, it was removed every week because I'd never seen it before.

"Faith, what are you doing?"

Startled, I turned to face my father. He was too close for me to hide the flyer. It only took him a moment to recognize it. "By all means, take that trash down and throw it away. Those people — we have to check the board vigilantly." The street door opened and several parishioners came in. "Put it in your pocket out of sight, for heaven's sake."

I did as I was told, folding the flyer into a small wedge and slipping it into the pocket of my sweater. Even when I was settled and clearing my mind to take Communion, which I felt I sorely needed, the flyer burned a hole in my pocket. I fancied I smelled sulfur.

With Eric still away, I found myself feeling rather low over the next several weeks. I began spending more time in my apartment making notes on my books and not going into my office every single day. I took pleasure in grocery shopping and making my apartment into a home, but I felt unsettled and out of sorts. James gave me a particularly vicious tongue-lashing for being what he called an indolent sloth.

Not having seen Sydney, I was able more and more successfully to forget how she had made me feel. And I did miss Eric. We'd gotten quite comfortable with each other.

He called me toward the end of his business trip just to say hello and explain that he had to stay in Hong Kong another week.

"Let's plan to do something fun on Halloween, though. I'll be back in plenty of time."

"I'd love to. I have a hankering to dress up like Eleanor just to get the feel of it," I admitted. "Something like what Katharine Hepburn wore in *The Lion in Winter*."

"I'll be Peter O'Toole, then."

"You have to yell a lot," I said. "Henry liked to address people at the top of his lungs." I pictured Eric in chain mail and a leather jerkin. He would look the part, except that he didn't have a chance of duplicating the swagger and sweat O'Toole had put into his portrayal of Henry.

"It's a date. Who knows where we'll go, but it sounds like fun."

We chattered for a while about football, a passion of his I was beginning to share, then he said he had a few more calls to make and then he had a meeting with his clients and their general contractor.

About five minutes later the phone rang again.

"Faith, this is Sydney. I'm on pain of death from Eric to make sure you're doing fine in your new apartment."

Her voice, light and friendly, shook me in an instant back to that moment at the pool table and her arms around me. It was as if I hadn't spent the last month putting her out of my mind.

"I'm doing fine, really. I was just talking to him."

"He said he thought you sounded a little lonely and insisted I take you to dinner in his stead."

Irony is only funny when it happens to other people. I opened my mouth to say she really didn't have to worry and heard myself say instead, "That sounds wonderful. I'm getting tired of my limited cooking repertoire. I'm not in your league at all."

"I'm hardly cordon bleu. Can you make it this Friday night?"

"Yes, that would be great. Shall I meet you somewhere?"

"At the City Club. It's on the thirteenth floor of the Wrigley Building. Let's say seven-thirty. Don't worry if I'm late. They'll seat you and ply you with delicious little things to eat until I get there. Though I'll try not to be late," she added. "It's just that things come up."

"I understand. And I'm glad you called. It is nice to have something to look forward to."

She hung up with a cheery good-bye, and the phone rang again almost immediately.

"Faith, it's Caroline Van Allen. I hope I'm not calling too late."

"Not at all," I managed. Why on earth would Eric's mother be calling?

"I was just talking to Eric. He told me you and he had a desire to do fancy dress for Halloween."

"We decided it would be fun," I said, wondering where this was leading.

"I'm having a fundraiser at the house on Halloween — so nice that it's a Saturday this year. I'd love to have you and Eric join us. Fundraisers can be tedious sometimes, and family makes it more fun. In fact, I was hoping to persuade you to come up for the weekend with Eric. He speaks of you often, and I'd like to meet you. My husband is a great admirer of your books, by the way."

I felt a little overwhelmed, by her friendliness and my total lack of preparedness for the step of meeting Eric's parents. "That sounds like more fun than I deserve, so I'll say yes. If it's okay with Eric," I added anxiously.

She laughed pleasantly. "It's fine with him. He was quite excited at the prospect. If I'm lucky, I'll be able to get Syd up here as well. He said you got on famously."

"We did," I admitted. Irony really is only funny when it happens to other people. How was I going to be able to face this? "In fact, we're having dinner on Friday."

"Lovely," she said. "And I'm delighted you'll join us at Lakeview for Halloween weekend. It should be fun. Other than the party, we'll be pretty casual. Eric wouldn't think to tell you."

"Thank you," I said. What on earth was *pretty casual* for the Van Allens? Eric's idea of casual wear was a sweater that cost my monthly rent. Don't panic, I told myself. It was too late to worry about not being rich.

"We'll see you then, dear. I'm so looking forward to it."

I stared at the phone after she hung up, numbed by the enormity of my predicament. Caroline had been truly friendly. But meeting Eric's parents, something that would have delighted me two months ago, was now vastly complicated because Sydney would be there.

I told myself sternly that if I couldn't manage a weekend, there was no way I could manage a lifetime. It would be the final test. I had suppressed these feelings before and would do so again. I would start by having dinner with Sydney on Friday. Everything would be fine.

Even as I convinced myself of this, my gaze went to two pieces of paper on my desk. The name and number Nara had written down for me. And the Dignity flyer. Abruptly I got up and put them in the drawer. But I didn't throw them away.

"John, I'm sorry, but I'm late for a dinner engagement. I just can't!" Sydney hadn't meant to be so forceful, and John looked at her in surprise. "I'm sorry, I'm sorry. I'm just tired."

"You've been different lately, Syd." John didn't believe in beating around the bush.

She stood up and started packing her briefcase. "I know. I'm keyed up about this nomination. I'm starting to remember why I decided not to run for alderwoman again. It's sta-ress-full."

"That's not all," John said. "There's something else. You don't have to tell me, but I wanted you to know it shows."

Sydney bit her lower lip. "Thanks. Don't worry, the Ice Queen is still here."

"She doesn't have to come back —"

"Oh yes she does," Sydney said, quickly. "My life

was a whole lot simpler before . . . well, it's just easier if I stay focused. I had to call my sponsor last week, and it unnerved me." She clicked her briefcase closed.

John put his hand on her shoulder as he stood up. "I'll try to lay off for a while, then."

"You're a slavedriver, John. Keep it that way."

"I forgot you had limits."

Sydney hurried to her office door saying, "It's forgetting the limits that gets me into trouble. Lock up, okay?"

"You got it."

She waited impatiently for the elevator. She wasn't actually late for dinner with Faith, but she wanted to go home and change. The mustard from the polish dog Cheryl had brought her for lunch adorned the lapel of her light gray suit.

Fortunately, the cab was quick and she had enough time to worry about the right thing to wear. Sweater and slacks seemed too casual for dinner. Another suit seemed too impersonal. She finally settled on black wool slacks with an emerald, high-necked raw-silk blouse and a black vest tied tightly in the back.

There. She was done. She looked at herself in the mirror and knew she had dressed for a date. Her trembling hands gave her away. But if she couldn't get through dinner, how could she get through a weekend without betraying how she felt about Faith? What if Eric married Faith? What then?

Even though Sydney had braced herself, she wasn't prepared for the obvious welcome in Faith's eyes. She also wasn't prepared for the simple black dress with a tight-fitting bodice that Faith was wearing. Sydney had the urge to shake her — didn't she have a clue about how lovely she was? An expressive face, and skin that old friends of Sydney's spent a fortune trying to buy. Didn't Faith realize she was driving Sydney to distraction?

"I just got here," Faith said. "You aren't late at all."

"No, but if my aide had his way, I'd still be chained to my desk."

"You can blame it all on Eric."

Yes, Sydney thought. This was all Eric's fault. For introducing her to Faith and for insisting that they have dinner while he was out of town. Eric and Faith were just too naive, she thought peevishly. Did they think she was made of stone?

Faith ordered an iced tea, and the waiter turned to Sydney.

"Two fingers of Glen," she said, and then literally gaped at what she had said. "No, Stanley, don't bring me that. Iced tea." Stanley smiled understandingly and melted as smoothly away from the table as he had arrived. "Jesus," Sydney said. "I haven't slipped in a long time."

"What on earth is Glen?" Faith rested her chin on her hand with a gentle smile that did nothing to settle Sydney's badly jangled nerves.

"Glenfiddich. The smoothest, easiest, single malt scotch whiskey on the face of the planet. Five generations of the William Grant family have been making it with love in Banffshire, Scotland, since eighteen eighty-seven. When waiters hover I reflexively want to order it. I did, thousands — I do mean thousands of times. But it's been a while since I actually ordered it."

"Too much stress, maybe."

"Stress?" Sydney tried to relax and match Faith's cool and calm manner. "I don't know what I have to be stressed about."

"A law practice, lots of pro bono work with a lot of people counting on you to help them, and a potential political campaign."

Alarmed, Sydney said, "How did you know about that? It's not a sure thing yet."

"A campaign? One of the professors I work with thinks you should be a state senator. I was actually teasing. I wanted to see if it was something you'd thought about." Faith was utterly without guile, and Sydney relaxed.

"I've thought about it. Other people have thought about it. But that's all."

"I'd vote for you," Faith said.

"Thanks," Sydney managed. The waiter delivered their iced teas and a tray of imported cheeses and crackers. "I would need all the support I can get."

"Would you like to order now, ladies?"

Faith looked puzzled and glanced surreptitiously around her.

Sydney smiled reassuringly. "No menus needed. Order anything you like. They'll have it. I'm having my favorite." She looked up at the waiter. "Filet mignon, medium rare, with the green peppercorn and mushroom glaze."

"The chef was just taking brioches stuffed with crab and lobster in a wine cream out of the oven. Would you like one to start?"

"If you don't, I will," Faith said. "It sounds divine."

"Let's split one," Sydney said. "Because I want potatoes mashed with garlic. And a double serving of broccoli for penance."

The waiter smiled and turned to Faith. "What may I get you?"

Faith seemed at a loss, then said with an impish smile, "I'll have what she's having. Except for the broccoli. Spinach salad?"

"Of course, madam. How about a sizzling bacon dressing on the salad?"

"Sounds wonderful," Faith said.

Stanley smiled genially at them. "I'll bring the brioche in just a moment. Can I get either of you a bowl of soup? I know there's leek and carrot, and New England clam chowder."

"I'll try the leek and carrot," Sydney said.

"Clam chowder would be perfect," Faith said when Stanley glanced at her. She watched him walk away, then turned back to Sydney. "Forgive me for acting like a peasant," she said, her mouth quirking. "I've never been to a place quite like this."

Sydney tried not to stare at Faith's lips, but was only partially successful. "I do like this place. I can wander in after a late meeting and get soup and a BLT at midnight."

"Is the wine cream okay? I hope that's not a stupid question," Faith said.

"You mean because of the alcohol? In cooking it's not a problem, at least not for me. The alcohol's long gone. I could probably even have a glass of wine, though I don't want to test that theory. Wine was never my problem."

"Single malt scotch whiskey made by five generations of Scots?" Faith's teasing smile made Sydney's nerves turn to honey, which made her all the more disgusted with herself.

"You got it." Sydney sighed. She'd been thinking about drinking too much lately, just like she'd been thinking about Faith too much. Both would get her in trouble.

"You know, Eric's told me very little about you." Faith sipped her tea and fixed Sydney with a serene gaze that Sydney envied.

"And I hope that it was all good." She launched into her usual bio speech. "There's really not that much to tell. I got my undergrad at Brown, master's — political science — at the JFK School of Government, and my J.D. at Harvard. Then I made up for being a model student by being spectacularly drunk for about three years, losing almost all my friends, nearly my family, and then I spent two years rehabbing and being generally dilatory."

"Sloth," Faith said, "is one of my favorite deadly sins."

"It was worse than sloth."

"Mendacity? Hebetude?"

Sydney laughed. "Hebetude? You're making that up."

Faith quoted primly, "Hebetude: noun. Dullness of mind. Mental lethargy."

"Remind me never to play Scrabble with you."

"You'd hold your own," Faith predicted. You read a lot, remember."

"I read about four books a week for two years. I didn't really sleep much. I didn't want to," Sydney admitted. It was hard to talk about that time with Faith looking at her so innocently. She could have no idea what kind of person Sydney had been. And Sydney wasn't about to enlighten her further. "After I got sober I started doing free legal work for a women's shelter that was being sued by an irate husband because they'd had him forcibly restrained by their security guards. The lawsuit had no merit whatsoever." She heard her voice becoming impassioned. It always did when she talked about that case. "It was my first case, and it wasn't a hard one, but I prepared as if I were arguing before the Supreme Court. I had to prove to myself I could do it. After that, I had all the requests for pro bono work I could handle. There's no shortage of need. After a couple of years I had my confidence back."

"After the rough start you had, it's amazing that you were elected to office so quickly. People's memories tend to be long."

"Long enough," Sydney said. "But I had an idea a lot of people liked, so they elected me. Measure D passed, and I went back to law. But since I've been in recovery, I've had to be extra circumspect. I get up every morning and tell myself that today I'm proving that I'm not the person I was. It means lots of work. Occasionally I get to relax."

"But no love life?" Faith looked suddenly tense as she asked that, and Sydney decided that Faith knew she was gay but wasn't particularly comfortable talking about it. She was twisting her napkin — no, not comfortable at all.

"Absolutely no love life. Not only would it distract

me from my work, it was too closely wound up with drinking. I don't know if I started the one that I wouldn't start the other," she said, hoping she wasn't being too oblique.

Apparently not. Faith nodded slightly and stopped twisting her napkin. Just then Stanley brought the brioche, the core of the hollowed-out bun spilling out chunks of crab and lobster in the aromatic cream sauce. He expertly set out the requisite plates and knives and urged them to enjoy it.

Faith said with a laugh, "Can I come to dinner every night?"

Sydney could only smile, and she hoped it hid the dismay she was feeling. Because her body answered Faith's question quite seriously. "Yes," it said, emphatically enough that Sydney had to clench her thighs and press one hand to her stomach.

"I'm starving," she said. It was far too true.

6

I am poured out like water . . . my heart is like wax.

— PSALMS 22:14

I didn't remember very much specifically about dinner. The food was delicious, of course. Sydney was amusing, and we talked about art and politics — getting along famously, as her mother had put it. But whenever I wasn't completely absorbed with either the food or conversation, I reminded myself that I had no future with her except as Eric's wife.

She would be a good friend, I told myself. She was obviously honorable and dedicated and had come to an understanding of herself after a great struggle. Her strength of character was as much a part of her as the color of her eyes. It was also obvious that she had set aside a personal life in favor of law and politics. As she discussed a couple of particularly intricate cases, it was clear that she believed sincerely that if she unwaveringly did the right thing justice would eventually prevail.

"If you do become a senator, won't it be difficult, having to trade votes? Isn't that how politics works?"

Sydney looked up from her dessert, a chocolate-caramel torte. "I found that hard when I was an alderwoman. In fact, it keeps me uncertain about being a senator. I will have to vote for things I normally wouldn't favor in return for votes on issues important to me. I can only hope that I keep my eyes on the greater good and not the game of trading. For some people the game is all that matters. They hardly care about what happens to the people, and that's the reason I'm there."

My hazelnut cheesecake with bittersweet chocolate lace was almost gone. I felt only mildly ill considering the meal I'd just eaten, but it was a pleasant kind of ill. Gluttony, another of my favorite deadly sins. "There's a similar ethic among some academics who are more concerned in securing awards and grants than in the study itself. The university encourages it, too. I've as much as been told that a *New York Times* best-seller might loosen the coffers enough for research assistants and grants so I can write more — to the greater glory of the university. I might be able to move from teaching in the college to teaching university graduate students in history."

I savored my last bite of cheesecake. "Of course if I don't do my own research, then the insights it would give me would disappear and I wouldn't produce what I felt was the same quality of work. My goal is to add insights to history, not write two or three books a year. Of course I'd like to be teaching graduate students, but I can live."

Sydney swallowed the last of her torte with a satisfied smile. "I heard a joke once about the university. They're so eager to lengthen their list of Nobel laureates affiliated with the University of Chicago that they put Henry Kissinger on the list because he stopped to ask directions."

I snickered. "That joke has been around a long time and I think it's true. Not that there aren't fine scholars at the university —"

"Present company included," Sydney said.

"You'll make me blush," I said. "If I'm not already flushed with all this food."

"You've got no ego to speak of, have you?"

"So I've been told. But I do. It's just not flashy." I glanced at my watch. It was after ten.

Sydney misread my meaning and said anxiously, "It's getting late. I hope it's not too inconvenient. We could leave right away."

"Oh no, we can take our time. That is, if it's okay with you." I had finished my cheesecake but still had my espresso, which had just reached the right temperature.

"Actually, I was thinking we might see what's playing at the Water Tower cinemas. There should be at least one more showing of everything at this hour."

I told myself a whopping lie, that it was of no consequence to me whether we prolonged the evening. At least lying wasn't a deadly sin.

About fifteen minutes later a cab was taking us the eight blocks or so to the Water Tower. We made our way to the theater only to be disappointed at the selection.

"Violence, violence, Disney, more violence, teeny-bopper slasher, seen it, and really bad reviews." Sydney chewed her lower lip. "I didn't know there was a *Lawnmower Man One*, let alone a *Two* or a *Three*."

"None of these is going to be around at Academy Award time."

"What a shame," Sydney said, biting her lip. "I was looking forward to a movie."

"So was I," I said. Well, not so much to a movie as to more time with Sydney.

I tried to call back the thought, but it was too late. I had forgotten to lie to myself. Still, it was only one of few slips for the evening. So far, so good. Perhaps it wouldn't be a bad idea to go home, though. Sitting with Sydney in a darkened theater, feeling the heat of her body only inches from my own — lying might not be a deadly sin, but lust most certainly was.

"How about popcorn and pool at my place? Or table tennis?"

"Honestly, if I ate anything, I'd be sick. Really." That was no lie.

I was about to add that pool sounded like fun, when Sydney abruptly seemed to change her mind. "Let's call it a night, then," she said, quickly. "I've just remembered I have a breakfast meeting."

I agreed, trying to look happy despite the sudden depression I felt inside. She insisted that we take one cab so she could see me safely home, allowing her to give a complete report to Eric.

Eric. This was all getting too serious and too twisted far too quickly.

Eric got back from Hong Kong the third week in October. He had been working almost nonstop on construction supervision. He would have to go back for several more weeks around Thanksgiving.

From the moment I saw him I felt myself divide into two people. I returned his warm hug and gentle kiss without a second thought. Another part of me compared his kiss to Renee's devouring passion and speculated how Sydney's kisses might feel. I felt no tension, only a kind of distance.

We had dinner, then drove all the way to Aurora where an art theater was showing *The Lion in Winter* on the big screen. I found myself sighing in the memorable scene where Eleanor examines her fading charms in a bronze mirror. The nearly sixty-year-old Hepburn never looked more beautiful to me. Her eyes were windows on the character she was creating. Henry called her conniving, deceitful, and manipulative. I preferred astute, political, and determined.

As we were leaving the theater, Eric asked, "Where are we going to get these costumes?"

"I know someone who is in the SCA. I'll bet she knows where we could get them."

"SCA? Some Costumes Available?"

I laughed. "Society for Creative Anachronism. It's a role-playing social club where people create characters from medieval history and dress up and have parties and are very particular about accuracy."

"That actually sounds like fun."

"I've thought about joining, but it can be time consuming. Not to mention the required schizophrenia." I was growing more familiar with schizophrenia as the evening progressed.

"So you'll check that out? Let me know if I need to do anything. I'm glad you're going to come up to Lakeview for Halloween weekend. I think you'll really enjoy it."

I assured him I would, and part of me believed it while another part knew Sydney would be there. I asked him in to see my new apartment, and he gave it smiling approval, saying its simplicity suited me. Contrary to my mother's expectation, he did not try to ravage me. We enjoyed a cup of coffee, and he took his leave with one of his usual gentle kisses.

Even as I told myself that we'd had a pleasant evening, I was walking to my desk, opening the top drawer, and taking out the Dignity flyer. The very nice man who answered the twenty-four-hour hotline gave me the address of the next support group meeting. I went to bed, feeling like a sleepwalker.

I had lurid, childhood-type nightmares in which flames, horned demons, and the thundering voice of God (sounding very much like my father) boomed at me in a language I didn't recognize but understood. One phrase was clear: *It is an abomination*, repeated again and again. In the morning I laughed at the images, chagrined that my psyche was so obvious.

I realized after my classes on Monday that I hadn't seen James since the previous Wednesday. He didn't answer his phone, and the English department

secretary told me he had called in sick. I then realized I'd never heard the results of his doctor visit, or
even if he went. It had been several weeks, and I
suspected that he had put it off again. When he came
into my office late in the day I was glad to see him.

"You don't look sick to me," I said. "Did you
have a nice long weekend?"

He made a face as he sat down, and I realized he
looked very tired.

"On the other hand, you don't look particularly
well," I said. "What's up?"

"I went to the doctor," he said. "He said I've still
got a few months to live."

I laughed. "And after that you move to Skokie?"

"Actually, the oncologist said two months. Maybe
three." He pressed his lips together.

I realized that he wasn't joking. "James . . .
what . . . ?"

"Don't get mushy on me. You know, my father
died when he was forty. Both of my uncles before
they were forty-five. I didn't expect much more, not
after the life I've led. I just thought I had a few
more years." His smile was ironic. "On the bright
side, I won't have to come here any more. Fuck
'em."

I managed through my very tight throat to say,
"What exactly is wrong?"

He looked at me with compassion as I tried to
maintain some semblance of poise. It felt as if my
throat would burst, and my eyes were stinging. Meg
could cry elegantly at the drop of a hat, but I had
never had her knack.

"Don't cry, you'll get blotchy. I have cancer of the
largely ignored organs. Like the spleen and pancreas.

Maybe even my liver. But I decided not to have the tests to find out. I've got to budget my time wisely."

I tried to stop the tears that escaped because I knew they would upset him, but I didn't have any success. "I'm so sorry," I gulped.

"Lighting candles won't help, but I need the prayers. So feel free. And I have a favor to ask."

"Anything," I said.

"Don't come to visit me. I'm going to get a lot sicker very fast. I'd hate it."

"So this is good-bye?" My head felt as if it would explode.

He didn't say anything, but rested his hand on mine for a moment before getting up to kiss me on the top of my head. Then he left, shutting my office door behind him.

I cried and tried to do a few things to stop crying, but would only start crying again. I realized after some time that it had gotten quite late and the faculty shuttle to the El had stopped running. I hardly cared. I'd take a cab home. It was safer anyway.

In a stupor, I gathered my things, called for a cab to meet me at the West Gate, cried some more, then managed to walk through the sharp evening air to meet the cab.

When I got home I turned on my new TV as a diversion, though I had no idea what I was watching. I badly wanted to call Sydney for comfort, and she was the last person I could call. So I sat, frozen by grief and guilt. I woke up in the middle of the night disoriented, then remembered James and crawled into bed with a box of tissues to cry some more.

Tylenol did nothing for the massive headache I

woke up with, and I didn't feel like eating. I skipped going to my office and instead found myself on the El to St. Anthony's.

I was early for confession and didn't have to wait. The old words came easily. "Forgive me, Father, for I have sinned. It has been two months since my last confession."

"Confess your sins, repent of them, and you shall be forgiven," came the low reply from behind the grille.

I bowed my head. "I have been having impure thoughts." How archaic that sounded. "I . . . I want to be with someone forbidden to me. Father, help me." My appeal came from the depths of my soul.

Compassionately, "You must tell me more, my child."

"I am seeing a man who may ask me to marry him. I care for him, but I don't love him. I am very attracted to someone else in his family."

"And this other man is unavailable to you?"

My voice trembling, I gave up my great secret. "It's not a man, father. It's a woman, his sister."

Anxiously, "Child, you know this is a grave sin."

"I know."

"Have you acted on your feelings?"

I had already confessed my affair with Renee. "I had this trouble once before, Father, and was absolved. This time, no, I haven't . . . acted."

"Do you repent of your impure thoughts?"

"I have wanted to Father, I have tried, but I still think of her. I had very sad news yesterday, and I longed for her to hold me —" My voice broke.

"I cannot absolve what you do not repent. You

cannot yield to this temptation. You are in peril of your soul."

"I know."

Firmly, "You must repent."

I bowed my head. I longed for absolution. But it would be a lie to say I repented my feelings for Sydney. What I felt grew daily and it was a bright thread in my life. "I cannot."

"You are not absolved. There can be no penance."

I sucked in my breath and fought tears. When I found my voice I said, "Father, a friend of mine is dying. He's only thirty-eight. Why is God doing this to him?"

"This is confession, my child. Your must look to your priest for guidance on God's will."

Blood was pounding in my temples. "Then I confess my anger at God for doing this to my friend. And I am angry that he gave me the ability to feel love for another woman only to tell me I must repent these feelings."

Sternly, "These feelings are not from God. They are the devil's temptation."

"Is it the devil's work to make me hate myself so?"

"Child, you must turn from this path. You must repent and be absolved."

"I cannot repent," I said in a fierce whisper.

"Then you cannot seek the grace of Communion until you do."

I didn't say any more, knowing I would not get what I so badly wanted: forgiveness and acceptance. It wasn't here. It never had been.

* * * * *

I had myself under control when I told Eric about James. He was sympathetic and sad for my sake. I realized that he and I had become emotionally very close, and I mentally flagellated myself for what I knew had been a deception all along on my part. But I didn't have the nerve to stop it. I wanted something to happen. I wanted affairs to be out of my hands. I didn't want to be responsible for hurting him, because I did love him, much as I loved my brother.

I made excuses to my mother to avoid going to Mass for two Sundays in a row and assured her — lying through my teeth — that I was going to Mass at the small church only a few blocks from my apartment. The lies counted so much less than the Big Sin I was guilty of. The Sunday before Halloween I avoided Mass again, though I could tell my mother was angry. I couldn't go back to St. Anthony's; when I'd needed solace there had been nothing for me. I heard nothing from James, and the sensation of impending doom — his and mine — was with me daily. Without the meditative grounding that attending Mass always gave me, I felt as if I were walking on tissue over a chasm.

As the weeks went by without any contact with Sydney, however, I had gained back some semblance of the self-identity I'd had before I'd met her. I had successfully convinced myself again that I was doing the right thing and thought that perhaps after the weekend at the Van Allens' I could go back to St. Anthony's and honestly say that I repented. Maybe I didn't feel passion for Eric, but I would. I was just letting a few meetings with Sydney give me foolish notions. And seeing Renee again hadn't helped. I could cope, I told myself. Halloween weekend would be my three days in the desert, and with them successfully behind me I could look forward to the life I told myself I'd always wanted and that God so clearly wanted me to have.

The Van Allen family wealth had its roots in shipping and railroads and was now supported by a vast real estate empire. The family home, Lakeview, was north of Chicago between Lake Forest and Lake Bluff. It was palatial, standing alone on two thousand acres bounded by a wide, tree-lined avenue on the west, the property of a son of an ex-president on the south, and Lake Michigan on the east. It was private, and the thick elms and oaks were the color of old money. To the north was an extensive garden that was the enterprise of Caroline Van Allen, carried on from Eric's grandmother. The gardens gave way to a wilderness sanctuary that gave way to a naval training station. It was a long, long way from the south side.

When we came into view of the house I said, "Last night I dreamed I went to Manderley again."

Eric patted my knee. "It's not that big."

"It's bigger than Hearst Castle," I said. The buildings were Georgian in overall appearance with imposing two-story doors to the main building and both of the wings.

A cheerful manservant greeted Eric as he got out of the car and waited until Eric had helped me out before getting in and driving the car around the back of the house. I looked after my weekend bag, and

Eric patted my arm. "Lance will put it in your room. Don't worry."

I glanced up at him and smiled wryly. "I have to admit, I'm overwhelmed. I didn't expect it to be so much like a castle." I thought that Eleanor would have appreciated the scale of the mansion and grounds; they were as large as any she had ever known. The gardens would have been farms and crops worked by serfs. The expanse of bright grass could have been a tournament ground.

"Don't be intimidated," Eric said in a whisper. "The king and queen are friendly."

And they were. After I'd been shown by a waiting maid to my room where I quickly unpacked, I met up with Eric again in the immense main foyer. All I could think about was how long it must take to dust the chandelier's hundreds of winking crystal pieces. He escorted me to the family sitting room, a long, brightly lit room with enough sofas and chairs for twenty and a huge fireplace at the far end.

His parents greeted me with charm and easy grace, making me feel comfortable in my simple sweater and slacks. Eric's mother, who told me to call her Carrie, was also in sweater and slacks. But where I was wool and linen, she was cashmere and raw silk.

Eric senior was in deep green wool slacks with a casual yachting cardigan over a starched white shirt. He immediately told me he had read both of my books and that he looked forward to talking to me about how I did research.

Dinner was a casual buffet, casual that is, if a buffet with beef Wellington and poached salmon filets is casual. There were a dozen other guests, some of them family but most involved in the setup for the party the following night.

I munched happily on a cherry tart and felt a warm glow inside for the first time in weeks. Eric's parents had obviously set out to welcome me, and Eric was more charming and genial than I'd ever seen him. I did love him, I told myself. He was literally everything a woman could want. I smiled as I watched his face light up as someone came into the dining room, then turned to see who had come in.

My pulse raced at the sight of her. She looked so strong and beautiful. Over Eric's shoulder her gaze met mine, and I managed a smile and used my fork to sketch her a salute of greeting. Carrie and Eric senior rushed as eagerly as Eric had to hug her, Carrie telling Sydney she was far too thin and Eric senior gruffly saying she'd been away too long.

"Just you, dear? You can always bring a guest, you know." Caroline was still holding Sydney's hand as she drew her to the buffet table.

"Just me. There's no one special, Mom." Sydney helped herself to salad.

"Well when there is, you know the door is open. No matter who." Carrie seemed too eager to make the point, and I realized that Sydney was looking at me in the reflection of the mirror above the buffet. She sent me a smile that said, "mothers!" and I responded in kind. Carrie's worrying was familiar to me, but I sensed she meant it far more for Sydney's benefit than her own. It was obvious she wanted to be sure Sydney was happy.

No empty seats were near me, and I was just as relieved when Sydney settled at the other end of the table. Eric was talking to his father, and Carrie disappeared in the direction of the kitchen. I chatted to one of Eric's cousins about skiing; rather, she chattered about going to Switzerland at Thanksgiving and I listened politely, making inconsequential observations whenever she paused for breath.

I amazed myself that I could maintain a rational conversation when part of me˙ was gibbering with fear. When I looked at Sydney I felt a fire in my nerves, prickling all over my body. Just the sight of her made all my lies and evasions crumple around me. I couldn't lie to myself for the rest of my life. Eric was too fine a person to have half a wife, even if, feeling as I did about Sydney, I could bring myself to marry him.

I didn't think I could do it. I was almost certain that if Sydney hadn't come along I would have been able to. Unless some other woman had made me feel this way. It was the women. It was not a chance thing. Renee had not been an aberration, I admitted to myself. I was . . . lesbian. There would be no absolution because I knew there was no cure. And while I might find the backbone to abstain from the temptation, I would never be able to say I repented being tempted.

The other guests drifted off to various pursuits while Eric and Sydney, along with their parents, drew me into a cozy sitting room for a pleasant evening of conversation. Eric senior was sincerely interested in my books and confessed to being a medievalist. He promised to show me his library some time during the weekend and offered any materials he might have for my research. I gathered that, since it was something he wanted to spend at least an hour doing, the library was not small.

The evening passed without remarkable incident, other than my heart racing occasionally and a frequent feeling of vertigo. I tried not to look at Sydney, and worried that she might suspect. She didn't seek out my company either.

My bedroom was delightfully European, and its diversion helped me get a good night's sleep. The Italian marble fireplace and large canopied bed distracted me from thinking about the predicament I was in. I pictured Eleanor, perhaps brushing her hair dry in front of the fire.

After breakfast Eric confessed that he had a conference call he couldn't get out of and said his mother would show me her gardens while he was busy.

"But I promise that's the last interruption," he said, with his usual smile. Like hot chocolate on a fall morning, his charm warmed my heart. Why couldn't I love this man as I ought?

"Promises, promises," I said as easily as I could manage. "I'm well rid of you anyway. I want to see everything, and I can't do it with you kicking pebbles and asking if I'm done yet."

Carrie laughed. "You do know him well, don't you?"

"He was dreadful at a Lincoln Park Zoo benefit."

I was shrugging into my Windcheater in the foyer

when I heard a light tread on the stairs. I knew who it was without looking. Eric's warmth paled in comparison to the rush of heat in my face and arms. Suddenly I felt as if I were standing in front of an open oven door.

"Hi there. Sorry I missed breakfast."

"You were up too late working," Carrie said, her brusque tone softened by the look of genuine caring and concern she gave Sydney.

"Unavoidable," Sydney said. "But now I can lolly-gag all day."

"Why don't you tag along with us, then," Carrie said. "I'm going to show Faith the garden. We can wait while you get something to snack on."

Sydney disappeared into the breakfast room, and Eric headed for his father's study. Eric senior appeared briefly in unmistakable golf attire, asked after my comfort, kissed his wife, and whisked out the door. Sydney reappeared with one of the fresh croissants that had been on the breakfast table, and the three of us left the house and headed north on a wide foot path. Already moving vans were delivering tables and chairs to be carried in through a high and wide set of French doors. I glimpsed a vaulted ballroom as we went by.

Carrie was a brisk walker. Keeping up precluded idle chatter, but Sydney and her mother exchanged family information while I trailed behind, taking in the beauty of the morning.

The lawn eased into oak trees, and beyond the trees was a meadow long enough for football. A gravel path skirted the meadow and led past a grouping of picnic tables and a huge fire pit. It seemed so far away from the rest of my life.

Soon I could hear the babble of children over a high fence covered with thick ivy. The fence was artfully woven among the existing oaks and maples, and we followed along the fence until we came to a maintenance gate.

"Good morning, Mr. Torres," Carrie called. "How many buses this morning?" Sydney and I paused at the gate while Carrie and a man hidden in the depth of a beekeeper's suit went over how many children were expected for the day and which bulbs had been brought in and which were mulched and whether the pruning of the white birches should wait until Indian summer had passed.

Some matter of concern must have come up, because Carrie gestured once, wildly for her, though it was just a flick of one arm. "Syd, I've got to go talk to the tree surgeon," she called. "Can you take Faith on a tour? I'll catch you up."

Sydney waved her consent. "They'll talk for hours," Sydney said, heading along the path that skirted the fence. "A hundred kids or so — not too many. We shouldn't be overrun. They're setting up a Halloween activity area in the main garden, so let's go over to the Moroccan garden, okay?"

I nodded my assent and followed her along the wide pathway. "Why just kids? Why not the general public?" I tried not to look at her and found myself instead noting the pristine crease in her blue jeans and the brilliant flash of her scarlet silk blouse in the sunlight.

"Follow me," Sydney said, and we walked around the inside of the fence to where more children were making their way into the heart of the garden. "Stand right here and watch."

The shoulder of her gray suede jacket brushed mine — I hated myself for being so aware of it. I couldn't take in the scene before me for a moment, but then I saw what Sydney meant.

A group of eight- and nine-year-olds came in from the main gates and around the planters of evergreens. They pushed and shoved, bickered and laughed as kids do, but when they came around the planters and saw the long plaza of brilliant colors, the flash of water in the fountain at the far end, and beyond that an open patio ringed with jack-o'-lantern lights, their mouths fell open. Arches crowned with different greens invited exploration of Old English, Japanese, Italian, and Moroccan gardens. Most of the kids went silent for a moment — then they laughed and rushed forward, even the ones who looked far too cool to think a garden would be any fun.

Two girls ran by us holding hands and giggling, their innocence and pleasure a tangible thing, bright and pure. Sydney took my arm and pulled me across the plaza toward the Moroccan garden, and for a moment I felt the sweet innocence of youth and took her hand.

"You have to see my favorite plant," she said, pulling me along. "It blooms in fall."

My palm tingled, and a searing happiness filled me. The sunlight was heavy with gold, and a light breeze redolent with the last of Indian summer lifted wisps of hair from Sydney's neck.

She showed me everything — the dormant rose-bushes, salvia in crimson and bright blue, the herb garden that made us both sneeze and giggle as we blew our noses. Then we ran to the long meadow beyond the main garden where annuals and perennials were being turned to seed for next spring. Beyond the plantings was a long meadow of tall grains — barley and wheat and other grasses left to go wild. Sydney told me it hid a game fence that kept the wildlife sanctuary's herbivores out of Carrie's plants.

As we walked through the tall grasses, tiny gold seeds dropped from the heavy pods onto my hair and shoulders. I looked up for a moment and watched the tapered stalks brush at the sky. I felt seeds slip into my shoes and down my shirt and told Sydney they tickled.

"I know," she said. She walked ahead of me with her arms out, brushing the tall stalks as she walked, creating a golden flurry behind her. She looked like an earth goddess. "We used to do this when we were kids. The grass seemed a mile high then."

We peered beyond the fence, but no wild creatures came out of the undergrowth to see us. As we turned back toward the garden, hidden from us by the wall of grasses, Sydney took my hand again with the same innocent gesture as before, but this time innocence fled me and I trembled.

"I'm sorry," she quickly said. "I — I shouldn't have."

"It's okay," I said.

She stood looking at me and I found myself lost in the velvet of her eyes. I couldn't say anything. I just looked my fill.

"I know better," Sydney said, biting her lower lip. "If I were Eric's brother I wouldn't just touch you like that — Eric might not like it."

"But you're not his brother," I said, puzzled.

She fixed me with her gaze again, and I saw her lips part with a soundless exclamation. "Eric hasn't told you, has he?"

"Told me what?"

"I'm a lesbian."

My body swelled, my skin trying to pull away from my bones, aching toward her, pulling me toward her, and I gasped, just loud enough for her to hear.

Her face flickered with a moment of anger, and then that passed as she realized I wasn't shocked. She realized what I was, what I was feeling, and she swallowed.

"It isn't just me, is it?" As she spoke I noticed a pulse beating in her throat and my lips trembled. "Dear God. I thought it was just me. I came home this weekend so I could get used to you being with Eric. So I could put my . . . feelings in the proper category. But it's not working."

"It's my fault," I said, the words breaking out of me. "I shouldn't feel this way. I can't help it. I don't want it. I've never wanted it."

"But you can't help it. Don't do this to Eric," she said softly.

"I won't. Not feeling this way."

"Don't do this to me," she said, as if I hadn't spoken.

"I'm not doing anything to you," I said.

Her hands came to my face and she cupped my cheeks. Her thumbs brushed under my closed eyes. I could tell she had stepped closer, my arms sensed the heat of her. I knew when she kissed me it would burn, and I might never recover.

"You look at me that way," she said, her warm

voice coating my ears as I kept my eyes tightly shut against the glow of her, "and it makes me want what I've given up. Women. You."

I was shaking as if chilled to the bone, but my body was rippling with fire. Her thumb brushed a tear from my cheek. Into the whisper of the grain stalks moving in the breeze I said, "Don't make me beg. I can't do that again."

"Oh no," she said, her tone so alarmed I opened my eyes. "I wouldn't." I felt her fingertips tremble.

I said, "Kiss me."

My body rose to hers, and I felt as if I was coming out of my old skin and into the fresh new life of her arms. Coming home, coming alive, she seared my bare defenses as her arms came around me and then her mouth found mine.

I was hungry for the taste of her but was surprised by the sound of our kiss — my heart hammering in my ears, her low moan, my startled breathing, her fingers brushing down my face. Each sound so small, but they filled me with passion as fiercely as the pressure of her mouth and the warmth of her lips.

She kissed me again, and our mouths opened to each other, drinking deeply and sweetly until she drew back. A breeze stirred the grain, and a dusting of gold drifted over us. I couldn't take my gaze from her lips — peach with golden glints now — and this time I went to her and kissed her with all my pent-up need, then more softly as emotions were stirred that I hadn't experienced before — nothing like what I felt for Eric, and nothing like what I had felt for Renee.

"Faith," she murmured against my mouth. She pushed me away, then pulled me into another kiss as if she couldn't help herself. "Good God, what are we doing?"

She kissed me again. I pulled her to the ground, and through the flurry of gold I saw the vivid sky and reached up to pull it down over us. Safe and warm in her arms with her heart pounding against mine.

I lost track of time in those breathless, heady kisses. With a laugh of joy, she rolled over and pulled me on top of her, then drew my head down to hers, her lips calling mine. In this golden place, outside of time, I knew what I was and what I wanted. I wanted her. I shyly caressed her arms, and the softness of her ribs as we kissed. Sensing that she would not stop me, I lightly ran my hands over her breasts. They fit in my palms as I had thought they would.

Less shyly, she unbuttoned my blouse. I welcomed her mouth with a sigh of delight. She slipped my bra straps off my shoulders and kissed the newly bared skin.

"It's like I thought it would be," she murmured. "I knew your skin would taste like this."

I said the first thing that came into my mind. "You're melting me."

She looked up with a smile. "Am I?"

I nodded, feeling inarticulate. "It's the heat of your eyes."

She smiled again, and the velvet brown went purple. "I'll try not to burn you."

I pulled her mouth to my breasts and whispered, "You already have."

She went rigid, her lips so close to my skin I felt the tingle of her breath. "Oh Jesus."

"What?"

She looked up at me. Her eyes had gone brown again, a dark brown full of trouble and indecision. I wanted to pour myself into them and trembled when she licked her lips nervously. For a moment she inclined her mouth back to my breasts, then she rolled onto her side, covering her eyes with her arm. "Jesus," she said again.

I looked down at my half-naked body, dusted with golden seeds except where her mouth had been. With shaking fingers I rearranged my clothes and then looked at her. Her fists were clenched and her entire body was taut as a bowstring.

"Sydney," I said softly. I put my hand on her hip. "It's okay."

"Don't," she said violently, rolling away. "I can't. I don't ... Eric's in the way," she said. "I can't do this to him. And I ... I don't need this right now. I —" her breath caught with a half-sob. "I promised myself I would have a personal life sometime in the future. After I get the party nomination. After the election. After I make a difference. I can wait." She looked at me. "Oh damn. You don't want me. You can't want me."

"I do," I said quietly. "But this isn't going to work. I mean it would. Right now." I looked down at the crushed grass and grain. "Right here. But not after."

She rolled onto her feet and offered me her hand. I thought it more prudent to ignore it and scrambled to my feet.

"We can't do this," she said.

"No," I echoed. "We can't."

We stood there for a long moment, and I knew I couldn't be the one to turn away. Finally, Sydney said, "We'd better get back," and she led the way through the swaying grain, a flurry of fool's gold in her wake.

7

Many waters cannot quench love, neither can the floods drown it.

— SONG OF SOLOMON 8:7

"Help me get this thing on," Eric demanded.

I stood back to let him into my room and laughed as he tried to get the inflexible chain mail over his head.

"You'll lose an ear if you do that," I said. "Here, there are clasps on the right side. Then you can put your head through. Now you know what squires were for." I tugged the mail down on his broad shoulders. "I need some help myself. I can't get the wimple quite right."

Eric yelped. "Let me get my shirt into place — this stuff scratches like hell."

"Now imagine getting on a horse and riding for five or six hours to battle."

"That's so comforting." Eric grunted and rotated his arms to settle the chain mail. I stepped back to admire the final picture. He hadn't shaved in almost a week, giving him a close beard and a slightly devilish look. He looked like a medieval lord with hose and a fine silk shirt under the chain mail.

"You look good in hose," I said, teasingly.

He looked at himself in the full-length mirror and wiggled his toes. "I left the shoes and the tunic, but I can manage them alone."

"Then help me," I said. I had managed to get into the heavy, white damask dress. It was a simple design that fit snugly to my breasts and fell without waist to the floor. I had also managed to get the dozens of bracelets on. The heavy cabochon emerald earrings were rapidly stretching my earlobes. I hadn't realized paste would be so heavy. The real thing would have killed me.

I was thankful for my hair being both short and thick. The bobby pins holding the crimson kerchief on top of my head would stay in place. "I need the kerchief attached to the small snap on the back of the dress. Then wind it around and fasten it again — here."

Between us we finally managed to get the long piece of silk attached to my hair, draped over one shoulder with the corner ending at my wrist where it belonged, then caught through a series of loops to be attached to itself on the other side of my head. This final catch could be undone to show my face. When it was in place, the kerchief veiled my face from the point of my nose down.

"Very regal," Eric said. "And modest."

"Eleanor was never accused of being modest," I said, jangling the bracelets. "Did you know that when Richard Lion-Heart became king, Eleanor really ruled England? She was fifty-four at the time." When I wasn't thinking about Sydney, I was thinking about Eleanor.

"I can't wait to read your book, sweetheart. I know it'll be great."

We made quite a picture, standing side by side. It could have been so perfect, except that the eyes that stared back at me were eyes I'd never looked deeply into. I didn't know myself anymore, but I knew enough to know the picture was a lie.

I didn't know what I was going to do about it.

Carrie had told me that twelve hundred people were attending the party, which was the limit of the ballroom. To each side of the main ballroom were large rooms with buffet tables; I hadn't really understood the expression "groaning with food" until then. The ticket price to the fundraiser had been five thousand per person, and no one seemed to begrudge a penny. Carrie hoped the Children's Defense Fund would get at least four million in proceeds.

I had never been to an event like it. Eric and I were announced as Henry the Second and Eleanor, king and queen of England. We met Henry the Eighth and Anne Boleyn almost immediately, and then Louis the Sixteenth and Marie Antoinette. Both

Anne and Marie had garish stitches in their throats indicating that their heads had been sewn back on. There were two George and Martha Washingtons and dozens of flappers and Gatsbys. There were Frankenstein monsters and Draculas, several stunning black cats, witches of all varieties, and at least two Vincent van Goghs — one with his ear and one without. I kept my veil up in keeping with the masks almost everyone was wearing.

The orchestra varied the music among waltzes, swing, and hit parade ballads. Eric complained that chain mail wasn't made for dancing to "Take the A Train," but he made an effort, and I danced with several of his friends. All the while I wondered what Sydney was wearing and if I would recognize her.

I ran into her finally, well after midnight, while I was raiding the buffet for cold water and several of the puff pastries with spinach and fontina. She was dressed as John Adams, the tight-fitting vest and breeches setting off her trim figure perfectly. Her long, full muslin sleeves and powdered wig made her the picture of Colonial romance. Though the outfit was masculine, there was no doubt that she was a woman, and I felt a clenching deep inside me far too pleasurable to be indigestion. She made me a deep, respectful bow, her sleeves billowing as she gestured.

"My queen," she said, without a hint of mockery.

"Oh stop that," I said. "You don't believe in monarchy."

"True," she said, straightening up. "I believe in revolution," she said passionately. "Independence from the tyranny of England."

"Piffle," I said. "You just want to get out from under the taxes."

"You wound me, lady!"

I feinted a stabbing motion with a toothpick, and she staggered back into the arms of one of the George Washingtons then faked a splendidly drawn-out death.

Eric appeared at my elbow and laughed. "Somehow I don't think we'd have won our independence from Eleanor."

I brandished the toothpick. "Not when I'm properly armed."

Sydney sat up. "Revolution!" she declared. She got to her feet, slapped George on the back and said, "Come on, fellow, I've got big plans for a vacation at Valley Forge." They disappeared into the crowd.

I started after her, then stopped, realizing she had left me as soon as she could do so. She didn't want to see me. And I couldn't see her.

Eric proffered a plate of chocolates. "I found these in the conservatory. There's an entire dessert buffet in there."

It was after two when I saw Sydney again, her wig slightly askew as she talked earnestly to a small group of men around her. I recognized some of the faces but couldn't come up with names. I drifted toward them, hating myself for wanting to be closer to her.

The group laughed, and one of the men took over talking. They were having a political debate about municipal bonds for affordable housing — in the middle of a very swank party. I smiled behind my veil.

Apparently Sydney was one of those people who are always working.

"I'll convince you yet," Sydney was saying when an ethereally thin woman dressed as Veronica Lake cut in and took Sydney by the arm.

"Syd, dear, I haven't seen you in ages," she said from behind long, blonde hair covering one eye.

Sydney went rigid and said in a markedly unwelcoming tone, "Patrice, what a surprise."

"It's been at least ten years. You don't come to the Club anymore." Patrice managed to make it sound like an accusation. She dropped her gaze to Sydney's empty glass. "I've run out of Scotch, and so have you. I think we should go find more."

The men shifted uncomfortably, and Sydney said coolly, "I don't drink anymore Patrice. You'll have to find it on your own."

"I don't believe you," Patrice said coyly. I realized then that she was very drunk but hiding it well. "Any more than I'd believe you stopped doing all the . . . other things you used to do."

Sydney lifted her chin. "You'll have to find someone else to have your fun with, Patrice. I don't believe in living in the past."

"Who's talking about the past? I'm talking about Scotch tonight and breakfast tomorrow. It'll be like old times."

"No, Patrice," Sydney said patiently. "There's no turning back the clock."

Patrice pushed Sydney away with a sudden, ill-tempered pout. "You're no fun anymore, Syd. You're boring. And rude. You never called." Patrice looked around as if she'd forgotten what she was saying. "I'll get a Scotch, okay?" She walked carefully in the direction of one of the bars.

There was a strained silence among the men with Sydney, then one, much older than the others, said, "Aren't ex-girlfriends a pain?"

They all laughed, and Sydney smiled ruefully but said nothing. I noticed then that she had gone pale while talking to Patrice because some color was coming back into her cheeks.

I headed for fresh air, ashamed at myself for eavesdropping. Obviously, Patrice had been someone from Sydney's drinking days and Sydney had broken those associations. I stepped outside the ballroom onto a flagstone patio. It was chilly, but the sky was clear and I looked up at the stars. They were far more visible here than in the city.

I shivered, not from the cold, but from the sudden image I had of Sydney in bed with Patrice. What I felt wasn't jealousy, but it was a strong pang. Oh, great. Envy, another deadly sin. Envy, lust, lying to thy mother, and coveting thy boyfriend's sister. I was racking up quite a list for my next confession. If I ever had a next confession. I left the patio for the cool, damp grass, torn between laughter and tears and afraid, truly afraid, of the future.

I walked to a nearby black oak, thinking the exercise would clear my head. My pace quickened, and I wanted to run. If I ran fast enough perhaps when I stopped my life would make sense to me. But my dress was not made for vigorous exercise, and I stopped when I gained the shadow of the tree. I turned to look back at the party and saw that someone was following me. The white wig gleamed in the moonlight like my dress.

She didn't say anything until she was standing next to me. Then she said, too casually, "Did you enjoy the little scene with Patrice?"

I blushed to the roots of my hair and was glad of the tree's shadow. "No," I said in a whisper.

"You can't do this to me," she said intensely.

Stung, I snapped, "Do what?"

"Be near me."

"I won't bother you again," I said, trying to act dignified. I had behaved like a love-struck schoolgirl, and dignity was hard coming.

"Please don't," she said coldly, looking toward the party. "I don't want anyone to think that there's anything between us."

"There's nothing," I said, trying to match her coldness. "Your political career is safe."

She whipped around to stare at me and moved closer. The velvet of her vest brushed my arm. Her voice lashed at my shaky dignity. "This is not about my career. It's about Eric. Remember him? The guy who keeps telling me how glad he is I like you? How happy he is that Mom and Dad seem to like you? Remember him?"

I gulped and managed to say, "He never leaves my mind. Never." I fought back tears.

"Good," she said, drawing herself up. "I hope you keep it that way."

"I'm not sure I want to." The words slipped out before I could stop them.

"What's that supposed to mean?"

"For every thought of him, I think of you a hundred times," I whispered.

"Faith, don't."

"I'll never have this chance again," I said. "I didn't want to be a . . . a . . . lesbian. I've been fighting it longer than you've been fighting alcohol. I've lost this battle."

She turned her head so her face was in shadow. "What about the war?"

I undid my veil and uncoiled the kerchief, tugging it free of the bobby pins. I held out the crimson silk. It fluttered between us. "My flag," I said. "I surrender."

Raising her hand slowly, she caught a fluttering edge, then all in a rush reeled in the fabric and reeled me into her arms. Her lips were cool as the night, but when she opened her mouth to me, her passion ignited mine.

We tumbled to the grass, a fevered tangle of arms and legs, rolling into the bundle of my kerchief and the yards of muslin in Sydney's sleeves. It billowed around me, and like in the field, we seemed to fall out of time.

This will be my only chance, I thought, over and over. I drew her hands to my hips and helped her pull my dress up. Her vest was off. My greedy fingers unsnapped her collar, then swept inside her shirt to discover she wore no bra.

She moaned when my fingertips found her nipples. She yanked my pantyhose down and I squirmed to help her, not caring that our haste ruined them, spreading my legs for her, aching and arching toward her, my mouth finding her breasts as her fingers came to my wetness.

She moaned again, then gasped as I guided her fingers into me. I was beyond stopping now. In ragged whispers I told her and told myself that I had forgotten how good this felt. Forgotten how right it felt, forgotten about the heat and speed of it. I had no words for the pressure and ache of it, and then I was consumed by the spiraling moments when the rapture peaked and joined with terror — I thought I would shatter from the drumming waves of pleasure.

The pounding in my ears finally subsided and the cool of the night prickled my damp skin.

"Faith," Sydney was murmuring into my ear. "Good God, Faith," she said over and over.

"It's okay," I said, shakily. "I'm okay." More okay than I had been in a long time.

She kissed me, at first tender, then demanding. I felt a fire in my mouth and knew that only the taste of her would put it out. I slipped my hands down her breeches, and she shuddered when she realized I wanted them off of her.

"No," she whispered. "Please Faith, I can't." Her hands were on mine, helping me push the breeches down. "Please," she said again. "I can't do this." She groaned as I pulled her into a kiss and I realized she was shaking. She pulled my hands up and trapped them against her. "No."

Even as she said it, she arched her back, and my head swam with the realization that her body was begging for my touch. I knew that it would take only the tiniest gesture on my part — trailing my tongue across her offered breasts, another kiss, my hands slipping under her breeches again — to crumple her resistance.

Was this how I had appeared to Renee? Saying no, but my body screaming yes? I knew there was a line that Renee had crossed, but now, for the life of me, I didn't know where it was. I realized for the first time how tempting it was to make Sydney yield. She would hate me for it the way I hated Renee.

With a sob I pushed her away. Her breathing was ragged as she wrapped the shirt tightly around herself and tied the collar. She sat up and scrambled into her vest while I removed the ruin of my hose and pulled my dress down. I could slip my bare feet into the leather-soled slippers and no one would notice. The kerchief was another matter.

Sydney's wig had turned sideways, and I reached out to straighten it for her.

"Don't! Don't touch me."

I snatched my hand back. "I won't."

"Can you manage on your own?" She lurched to her feet.

"Yes," I said.

She half-ran toward the house, veering off as she reached the light for the side entrance. I took a more oblique route until I had light from a window to examine the damage. My dress had escaped without grass stains, but one side of the kerchief was smeared. I shook when I realized it wasn't just wet with dew. I wrapped an arm over my stomach as a wave of desire hit me, and I knew I couldn't go back to the party without pantyhose.

How had I come to this state, I wondered. What would my mother say if she knew I was wandering around outside without underwear and smelling like sex? I waited for the follow-up wave of self-disgust, but it didn't come.

I rolled my ruined pantyhose into the kerchief, and picked my way around the outside of the house to what I hoped was the wing where my room was. I prayed I wouldn't run into anyone while I looked and smelled like a rutting animal. I gained my room without incident and stared at myself in the mirror. I was pale, and my hair was a wreck of bobby pins. I looked nothing like the woman who had stood here earlier. When I looked into my eyes I saw understanding and terror.

I repaired the damage as best I could — good enough to find Eric again and say goodnight. I took one last look and saw a smile of satisfaction lurking around the edges of my lips. Tonight I was more at peace than I had been in a long time. I was happy.

Tomorrow I would reap what I had sowed.

No one was in the dining room when Sydney finally went down the following morning. The dim thud of the tables and chairs being restacked in the moving vans and the definite sounds of a half dozen vacuum cleaners throughout the main part of the house hadn't been audible from the west wing where the family lived.

Relieved that Faith was not there, Sydney helped herself to coffee and tried to read the paper.

Her mind kept wandering, and always to the same place. To last night with Faith. She knew her parents expected her to stay to dinner, but she would find an excuse to leave before then. The least amount of time she spent in Faith's company, the better.

The bottom of her stomach dropped out as she remembered again the way Faith's mouth had tasted and the soft curve of Faith's breasts. The wet, vibrant feel of her. Sydney had been with a lot of women, though she didn't remember many very clearly. None of them had been like Faith, so open and receptive, so responsive.

And then Faith had been kissing her, the first kisses out of her own pleasure and gratitude, and then she had changed. Such a subtle difference, but one a lesbian couldn't mistake. Faith had been tasting Sydney's mouth with intent to taste elsewhere. Sydney had ached for Faith's mouth on her and still did. Even after Faith had pushed her away, Sydney had wanted to pull her down.

Fortunately, she hadn't. And Faith hadn't pressed. Sydney knew she couldn't look Eric in the eye, but it had been a victory of sorts that she had been able to stop.

That was a lie, she told herself. She hadn't stopped, Faith had. She had been ready to throw away all the years of work and all the years of living by a moral code for ten minutes with her brother's girlfriend. Well, that impulse was behind her.

It had to be.

Her musings were interrupted by her father and Faith, both in search of coffee.

"I've been showing Faith the library," her father said.

"It's quite amazing," Faith said, brightly. Sydney wondered how she could look so calm. Sydney's heart was beating triple-time. "He has two of the texts I've been waiting almost six months for via interlibrary loan."

"I'm happy to loan them to you." Her father seemed inordinately pleased with himself.

Eric came in yawning. "Is there coffee?"

"When isn't there?" Sydney found she could match Faith's calm exterior even with butterflies ticking her esophagus. "There's always coffee." She had the impression that Eric wouldn't welcome any loud noises.

"Sorry, I had too much champagne last night. My head is stuffed with wool. I slept in that damned chain mail, too."

"Now you really see the value of squires," Faith said. "Some lad who wants to be a knight someday is supposed to help you with your mail, especially when you've had too much champagne." Faith's calm appeared genuine, and Sydney marveled at it.

Eric yawned in response.

Her father said, "I hope you slept okay, Syd."

"I did," Sydney lied. "Not having had any champagne," she added in a sanctimonious tone.

"Shaddup," Eric said. He sipped his coffee. "I do this once every five years."

Sydney rustled her paper loudly, and Eric flinched. "See that you keep it that way," she said sonorously.

"You sounded just like my father," Faith said. "But you need to point at him. That's much more effective."

Eric senior laughed. "She sounded a little bit like all fathers."

Sydney smiled at her father fondly. "I do seem to

remember a speech about the fleshpots of Europe and avoiding dens of iniquity. I didn't pay much attention."

"You should have," Eric said.

Sydney gave him a pursed-lip glare, relieved to take refuge in lighthearted teasing. "Shaddup."

"Children," their father said, "be nice or go to your rooms."

"Actually, I have to do that," Sydney said. "I need to get going."

"Your mother will be disappointed," her father said. He looked disappointed as well.

"I'm cochairing a conference on homelessness in San Francisco, and I've got a lengthy call with the other chair this afternoon." She really was working on the conference, but having a call was a lie.

"When are you going to San Francisco?" Eric opened his eyes wider than they had been so far.

"The week before Thanksgiving," Sydney said. She suddenly noticed that Faith looked alarmed.

Eric turned to Faith. "Does that overlap with your trip?"

"I don't think so," she said. "I think we'll miss by a few days."

"What a shame," Sydney said as sincerely as she could manage. Now she knew why Faith was a little pale. Damn Eric anyway.

"But you could go a few days early," he said. "The days aren't set in stone."

"I don't think the curator could change his schedule," Faith said. "It was a difficult appointment to make." She turned brightly to Eric senior. "A small museum in San Francisco has managed to acquire tapestries that are restored copies of paintings which copied tapestries from the twelfth century. Even though they're like fourth-generation photocopies, I'll still be able to see the style, costumes, and faces. The curator has granted me a few days with them so I can write sketches and descriptions in return for copies of my work. It will help me capture the feeling of the time."

"It would be nice if you could see the town together, that's all," Eric said.

"You know these conferences, Eric." Sydney turned a page. "I won't have a moment to myself. You've been to enough of them."

"I'd just feel better if I knew Faith wasn't going to be completely on her own while she's there."

"I'll be fine, Eric. I went all over France last summer on my own." Faith got up to refill her coffee cup.

"Well, no matter when you go, you should stay at my favorite hotel. It's very comfortable and very safe."

"Yes, mother," Faith said, busy with the coffee pot.

Sydney glanced into the mirror and saw Faith looking at her. For a moment, Faith's expression was hungry and wounded, then it cleared and became serene. Sydney's stomach did another slow roll — an alarming sensation that would have been painful if it weren't accompanied by treacherous sensations in the lower regions of her body.

Dear God, she thought. The only way I can stop wanting her is to never see her again. If Faith doesn't break up with Eric, what will I do? Faith would have to break up with Eric. Last night had proven that she must.

Sydney looked through her lashes at her brother. She owed him her life. If Faith continued to see him, what would she do about it for Eric's sake? What would she do about it for her own?

While my years of dithering and self-deception might have been over, I decided the following week that I was a coward. I couldn't find a way to tell Eric I didn't want to see him anymore, and I shrank from telling my parents I wouldn't go to St. Anthony's again. I wanted to hide from everything.

I considered telling my parents at least nine different lies because I was scared to tell them the truth: I am a lesbian and therefore outcast from our church. And I had no illusions that they would accept me as Sydney's parents had obviously accepted her.

I now went to my office at the university only on my teaching days or for faculty meetings. Without James to spar with, I felt disconnected from everything except my classes, which continued in their usual pattern, though this quarter there seemed more uninterested freshmen than usual. I contemplated buying myself a computer for home and forgoing my office on campus for anything but student meetings, but that seemed like a big decision. I was all out of the energy big decisions required. I managed day by day, making very small decisions that avoided Eric and my family altogether.

When I got home on Friday there was a message on my answering machine from a Terry. He left his number and even though I didn't know him it was plain he knew me. I called back and I thought about what I'd have for dinner while the phone rang.

"Hello, this is Terry."

I didn't recognize the voice. "This is Faith Fitzgerald. You left me a message."

"Oh right, Faith. I'm a friend of James's. I'm sorry to tell you that he died this morning."

Died. James was dead. It had only been a month.

"Faith, are you still there?"

"Yes," I managed. "Thank you for calling me."

"It happened much quicker than anyone thought. He was lucid yesterday and then last night he had a heart attack and a series of strokes and it was like his body just gave up all at once. He only spent last night in the hospital, and that's really what he wanted."

"Will there be a service?" I felt like lead.

"Sunday at two-thirteen."

I smiled at James's habit of setting times on the odd minutes. He said they never got enough attention. My throat tightened as I realized I really would never see him again. Even though I had known it was hopeless, it's human to hope. The hope I had secretly hoarded that he would get better flickered out.

Terry told me the name of the church and assured me there was nothing I could do. His friends were taking care of all the details.

I called my mother after that and begged off one more Mass, this time without a lie. For the first time in my life I really didn't care what she thought of me. Nothing to lose, James. You were right.

* * * * *

"I wrote it in my calendar, and you will be in San Francisco at the same time as Faith. I'd go with her myself, but it would look all wrong. She's old-fashioned and her reputation matters to her."

Sydney glared at the phone as if it were Eric. "You're pretty old-fashioned yourself, you know. Eric, it's not that I don't like her, but I got the feeling she's looking forward to having some time for herself."

"Just one evening," he wheedled. "Syd, it's important to me that you like her. I, well, I think we have a future together."

Damn Faith! This was so unfair to Eric. He didn't know he was being the serpent, dangling the Faith-apple in front of his still and constantly tempted sister. "I'll call her," she promised. "But if I get the idea that she wants to be on her own, I won't pursue it." And if she does agree to have dinner in San Francisco, I'm going to give her a big piece of my mind. She's got to break with Eric, and soon.

"Fair enough. I've got another call. Talk to you later."

Eric rang off, and Sydney pouted at the phone. She heaved a sigh and then realized that John was watching her from the doorway.

"I've got the new draft," he said, setting a two-inch stack of papers on her desk.

"Thanks," she said, watching him watch her.

"We can't all like our brother's choice of girl-friend, you know."

"Eavesdropper," Sydney said, too weary to put any

snap in her voice. "It's not disliking her that's the problem."

John's eyebrows went about halfway up his forehead. "I think I see. You really like to grow blue corn, don't you?"

"Pardon me?"

"It's an old Hopi story. When corn was given to the various tribes, the Hopi asked for the blue corn. It was hard to grow and not very nourishing, but they felt it would give them character."

Sydney shook her head tiredly. "If I had any more character I could cast a Cecil B. DeMille movie on my own. I'll get over it."

"*Chica*, you'd better."

"Oh get out already. I need to make a call."

John left at his usual pace. He reminded Sydney of Duchess sometimes — the more Sydney said jump, the less likely it was he'd even move.

She hoped she'd get Faith's answering machine, but after a few rings an odd-sounding Faith answered.

"I know this is awkward," she said after strained hellos. "But Eric knows we'll be in San Francisco at the same time and will want an explanation if we don't get together. You need to talk to him, Faith."

"I know," Faith said. Her voice was not quite right. "Why don't you tell him we will get together. Before we go I'll talk to him, and then he won't care what I do. I just can't talk to him right now."

"I won't lie to Eric. I won't. The first promise I made to myself when I got sober was that I'd never lie to him, because if I did my life would be in pretty bad shape. And it isn't." It was, she thought. But Faith didn't have to know that.

"I'm sorry," Faith said, then she sniffled.

"Are you okay, Faith? You sound odd."

"I'm all right. I just found out that a friend died. I feel like everything's coming unraveled, particularly me. I just can't talk to Eric right now. I have too much to think about."

"I'm sorry," Sydney said. She fought down the urge to drop everything so she could dry Faith's tears. An urge that was not in the least sexual, and was all the more dangerous. Lust was one thing, and it was proving a real bitch to handle. Having other feelings . . . absolutely not, Sydney told herself. There was no room in her life for any kind of relationship, even if Faith were available.

"Thanks. I will talk to him. I don't know . . . if I'll tell him the truth. I just don't know."

"That's your decision," Sydney said.

"No matter what, I won't mention you."

"I know you won't. I won't either. He's going to be crushed enough."

"I don't want to ruin things between you."

"I know." Her intercom beeped. "I have to go."

"Good-bye then," Faith said shakily, and she hung up.

Sydney hadn't realized it would be good-bye. She was swamped by a wave of loss. Then she felt hollow. She felt as if she was the one with a dead friend. It was familiar, this emptiness. There was one so very easy way to fill it.

8

I will not be ashamed to defend a friend.
— APOCRYPHA, ECCLESIASTICUS 22:25

If you pay in cash, no one will ever know how much or what you drank. Sydney's rule number 15. It came just after A moving Sydney gathers no girl-friends, and just before If she doesn't drink Scotch, don't stay for breakfast.

Duchess blinked one suspicious yellow eye at her as Sydney settled into the big chair that Faith had liked. She warmed the lead crystal glass in her hands and stared at the bottle on the table in front of her.

Glenfiddich, in its trademark triangular bottle. So easy to pick up and pour. A deep brown bottle with a brown and gold label featuring moose antlers and heather. Special reserve, 80 proof and aged twelve years. The amber light from its depths promised her oblivion. It promised that when she woke up everything would be all better. It promised that she could forget Faith.

The glass warmed — an important part of the ritual — she broke the seal on the bottle and deeply inhaled the comforting, familiar aroma of her favorite Scotch. She remembered the sharp, throat-catching smell so well, and knew it hid the smoothness that would coat her throat and slowly spread to her shoulders, her breasts, her arms. She would feel the warmth in her stomach and in her sex.

She breathed in again, letting it fill her head. Her sex didn't need any heat, there was plenty already thanks to Faith. She smiled and closed her eyes, remembering how delicious and easy sex had been when Glenfiddich had put her perpetually in the mood.

She filled the glass to the level of two fingers and then put the glass and bottle on the table.

So close. So easy. The mantra was so familiar.

If I drink, I'll forget about everything.

If I drink, I'll forget about Faith.

If I drink, I can be my old self again.

If I drink, I can call some old friends.

If I drink I can find someone to fuck and I'll forget about Faith.

If I drink, I'll forget about Eric. I'll forget about Eric loving Faith.

If I drink, I can be with Faith. I can be with Faith. If I drink, anything is possible.

She lost track of time, but not of her mantra. The glass was in her hand. No one would ever know.

There had been another mantra, learned at AA. It didn't seem to help now, but she began repeating it to herself. My name is Sydney and I'm an alcoholic. My name is Sydney . . .

Duchess flicked her tail, and Sydney realized she was speaking aloud. "My name is Sydney and I'm an alcoholic. Recovery is a lifelong journey. One minute at a time. One hour at a time. One day at a time. One week at a time."

One sip and she would have to start all over again, counting minutes, counting hours. She had just celebrated her ninth anniversary of sobriety. She trembled and knew she could not live those hard-fought nine years over again.

With deliberate steps belying the panic in her stomach, she took the glass and bottle into the kitchen and poured their contents down the drain, leaning back from the smell that suddenly nauseated her.

She would not, could not, come this close again. The only way to keep her sanity and sobriety was to get over Faith Fitzgerald. And she could do that by applying herself to her work and only her work.

She felt numb inside and heaved a sigh of relief. The Ice Queen was back.

I hadn't expected so many people to be at James's funeral. I had arrived just a little late and had taken a pew at the back of the Community Church Chapel. I recognized several other people from campus. The chapel was full, about a hundred and fifty or so. James had had a lot of friends.

The pastor, accompanied by an ensemble of about a dozen men with beautiful voices, led us in "Amazing Grace." I was too distraught to sing along. When we sat again, my vision was too blurry to read the program.

A friend read a poem about the cycle of life. Another played a short Bach organ piece that James liked. Had liked, I reminded myself. I gave myself over to listening to the pastor, who spoke from the chancel steps rather than from the pulpit. Close enough to the front pew to occasionally touch a hand or pat a shoulder. I hadn't been to a non-Catholic funeral in a long time and found the simplicity and closeness of the service refreshing and direct.

"Our friend James asked for 'Amazing Grace' because he identified so strongly with the words. He always spoke freely of his times of being a wretch, of his struggle with alcohol, and of a difficult family life."

He had never mentioned alcoholism to me. I was surprised and wished he had told me. But maybe he hadn't been so easy about it as Sydney. He had sometimes referred to estrangement from his parents. Well, I guess the measure of how well you know someone is whether you learn anything new at their funeral. I didn't know him as well as I had thought.

"He found that giving of himself for others helped him feel grace in his life. He was a generous and thoughtful person who loved to send cards on birthdays with a hand-penned, inimicable note."

I smiled. James would never tell me when his birthday was, but he had never forgotten mine. As vitriolic as he could be in person, in the last card he'd written, "Thank you for your treasured friendship."

"He raised over fifteen thousand dollars in the fight against AIDS through his willingness to join in walkathons and to twist the arm of anyone he knew for sponsorship."

The truth of that statement was borne out in the gentle laughter that followed it. I found myself smiling. He'd twisted my arm. My smile fled. I had paid him in cash because I'd been afraid my father would somehow see the canceled check. My father often said that while AIDS was a terrible disease, it was also a wage of sin. I was a coward, I reminded myself. Hiding my feelings from myself and my parents was second nature to me.

"James was notoriously witty. He referred to himself as vaguely normal, but with that his many friends disagree. There was nothing normal, or mediocre, about James. He was unique, and many of us were touched by him."

The service progressed with an a cappella version of the Twenty-third Psalm from the male ensemble, and I was greatly comforted by the beauty of the arrangement and the voices. I wiped my eyes and looked down at the program to see if it identified the group. The Chicago Gay Men's Ensemble, performing without one of their tenors, James.

I closed my eyes in shock, tears welling out from under my lids. I felt betrayed — why hadn't he told me? Didn't he trust me? Had I behaved in a way that had made him nervous? Not a word, not a hint, not a glance. Was I, in my silence, as bad as my father?

I lost track of the service and huddled in misery. I felt as if I'd never known him as I reexamined the friendship we'd shared. Could I call it friendship when he'd never told me this most important thing about himself? We'd squabbled and laughed, but always there'd been a distance. I'd thought the distance was in me, but now I knew it had been in both of us. The distance prevented us from really connecting, from having a friendship that was deep and lasting and that would comfort me now. Our silence made him a stranger to me. Now, instead of saying goodbye to him, I was berating him in my mind. I'd known so little about him that I felt I could now hardly call him a friend.

Mourner after mourner stood up and said how much they would miss him. Only then did I realize that men far outnumbered women in the chapel. Old lovers cried and put their arms around each other and perhaps I was the only person in the church who felt shock at the sight of men embracing so closely. I felt as if I'd lived in the cloister and was now moving at light speed into a world I didn't know. At St. Anthony's my father had arranged for several showings of *The Gay Agenda*. Even though I recognized the propaganda tactics of the video as it was shown, I was still repelled by the images. Men dancing naked in the streets, public sex acts. There was a lurid quality to the lifestyle that had made me all the more determined to put Renee behind me.

But these people were nothing like what I'd seen in *The Gay Agenda*. The men who cried for James weren't crying over lost sex. Two women with a toddler between them read a letter to James dictated by the little boy. It ended with, "I know you are in heaven and someday I'll visit you." I was not alone in my tears, and I finally realized that my head had been filled with preconceived notions about how gay people behaved. And because I didn't want to behave that way, I had kept myself from considering the possibility.

When I got home, I decided to call the number Nara had left me. As I suspected, Patrick Greenwood was a therapist. He was willing to see me the following Thursday and was pleased to hear that Nara had referred me.

I tried vainly to go to sleep that night. I couldn't sleep, not when I felt awake for the first time in my life. If I kept my silence about myself, my family and anyone who called me friend would go through what I had gone through today. Could I be so cruel? I knew James hadn't meant to be, and I had contributed to the silence between us. But on the receiving end it had hurt, and I was filled with regret and acrimony.

If I held back a piece of myself from everyone, who could truly mourn me? So many people obviously mourned James, from the depth of their souls and in complete understanding of his.

If I was not truly known by myself and my friends, would God know me? Could any God forgive a life that continued to be a lie?

Patrick Greenwood's office was in a small building on East Oakwood. I knew it was silly, but I was glad there was a mix of professions in the building. I had the irrational fear that someone who knew my parents would see me going in. My parents had definite feelings about therapists — that's what priests were for, they would say. But I'd already tried a priest, and after James's funeral my faith was deeply shaken.

He was younger than I thought he would be, mid-thirties. I had expected someone Nara's age for some reason. But he was clean-cut and all sincerity. We exchanged pleasantries as I hung my coat on the rack. The office was small and sparsely decorated but full of light.

"Nara told me a little bit about you, but why don't you fill in the gaps?" He opened a notebook as he spoke.

"You spoke to Nara?" Had Nara told him I was a lesbian?

"Since she referred you I called to thank her. All she said was that you and she had met recently." He looked at me with such an inviting and compassionate expression that I found myself speaking more easily than I had thought I would.

"I'm, well, she said you would understand what I'm going through. I was struggling with my sexuality." I felt myself turning red. "I've stopped struggling. I know I'm a lesbian. I'm not fighting it anymore."

He smiled gently. "Most of my clients come to me for help with the struggle. But you're beyond that now. What can I help you with?"

I had an overwhelming urge to call him Father. Transference and habit, I supposed. I tried to sound nonchalant and failed miserably. "What do I do now? I'm an outcast from my church. My parents will not want to see me, and I feel as if this mountain of retribution and anger will be coming down on me when I tell them." I twisted the strap of my purse.

"Do you have to tell them?"

"I can't lie. It hurts me, and it would hurt everyone in the end. I can't go to Mass anymore because I don't repent my feelings." I looked up at him. "Do you know anything about being raised Catholic?"

He nodded. "In fact, that may be why Nara referred you to me. I'm a recovering Catholic," he said with a rueful smile. "And I'm gay. I know what you're going through. The social disapproval is bad enough, but eternal damnation can be daunting."

I felt an enormous wave of relief. He did understand and had obviously found peace somehow. "Then you can help me, Father. I need guidance."

He abruptly sat back in his chair. "Why did you call me Father?"

I was confused, then realized what I'd done. "I suppose I'm just used to it. I won't do it again." I could see it had upset him.

"Forgive me," he said, lowering his head. "Give me a moment." I waited, feeling awful.

Finally, he looked up at me. "You hit a nerve. I wasn't just Catholic. I was ordained."

I gulped. "I'm so sorry."

"Don't be. You see, I still believe in penance, in absolution, and the sacraments. I've chosen to take a different path, and I believe that this . . . separation . . . is what God has chosen for me. But he won't make it easy. So the reminders I have of what I lost when I left the priesthood are painful. I think that's as it should be for me."

"What made you realize you couldn't be a priest?"

He smiled wryly. "I've never realized that. It was

a *who* that made me realize I was gay. A bishop decided I was no longer a priest. But I still feel the call. Every time I go to Mass I ache to celebrate it, but I can't. I am a good priest, with a lot to offer. Yet the Church chooses to waste one of its shepherds."

I bit my lower lip. "Will the Church ever change? There's so much condemnation in the Bible."

Gently, "Is there? What do you recall?"

"That it says homosexuality is a sin. An abomination."

He relaxed with a sigh, then gave me a reassuring smile. This was obviously familiar ground to him. "Not quite. There are only a few references to homosexuals, and they're all in the Old Testament. The New Testament is completely silent on the topic."

I hadn't realized that. "But the implication has always been that Christ condemned it."

"No. He didn't. He did say, Judge not, that ye be not judged. His commandment was that we love one another."

"The devil can quote scripture for his purpose," I said wryly.

"You'll have to decide if I'm a devil," Patrick said.

"I'll let you know," I said with a smile. "So where does it come from? I know there's something in Leviticus."

"Other than the reference to undescribed sins the men of Sodom committed, Leviticus is the only source for the church's teachings on male homosexuality. Two verses, forty-five words, out of nearly a thousand pages." He spread his hands. "Female homosexuality is not mentioned at all in the Bible. Perhaps, like

Queen Victoria, the original writers didn't believe it existed or could create any sinful pleasure."

Somehow I wasn't surprised. "The writers of the Bible largely ignored women. St. Timothy and St. Paul were explicit about the substatus of women. Omitting female homosexuals in the text isn't a loophole. You can't covet your neighbor's husband just because the commandment says *wife*." I thought for a moment, then went on, "I guess I have reconciled myself to the misogyny in the Bible, and popes over time have softened those teachings."

"A lot of what the Bible says has been modified and ignored in the modern church." Patrick tapped his pencil on his notepad. "Leviticus nineteen and twenty are the chapters with the two verses. To put them in perspective, Leviticus twelve says that a woman who has a male child cannot receive sacraments or touch anything holy for thirty-three days. Twice that for a female child. Leviticus seventeen tells us that the blood of all slain beasts should be offered at the tabernacle. Leviticus twenty-one tells us priests may marry; however, anyone with a blemish cannot be a priest. Blemishes listed include the blind and lame, flat nosed and crookbacked. In two thousand years, the Church has done away with many of the rules in Leviticus because they were outdated or supplanted by new teachings. For example, it took pressure from within and without to free some of my sisters in the church from virtual slavery and servitude to men in the Church. I think of those two verses in the same way and pray that someday the Church will recognize it."

I understood the comfort he was offering me, but didn't know if it would be enough to sustain me. I wanted to believe him. I wanted my faith again. People who aren't particularly religious don't understand how faith feeds the soul. "And if it doesn't, what happens to your soul? What will become of us?"

Patrick raised his eyes heavenward for a moment and his faith, not blind and unquestioning but faith nevertheless, was palpable. Thou art a priest forever, I thought. He was lit from inside in a way I hadn't seen in the older priests at St. Anthony's for many years. "Christ promised us that all things are possible to those who believe. He promised that our faith would make us whole."

My dread of telling my parents was as strong as it had been, but after seeing Patrick and talking with him for more than the allotted hour, I no longer felt as if I would wake up one day in Hell. He suggested that I look into the Metropolitan Community Church and other gay-affirmative churches if I wanted to attend services that would welcome me and still be rooted in Christian teachings. Dignity meetings, he also said, might be of help to me if I felt comfortable talking in a group.

Before I could even consider any of these options, I decided I would take one last Communion at St. Anthony's, to say what I had to say in my heart to the God in that church, and after that find my own way. Taking Communion when I hadn't received absolution was a sin, but I was past caring about rules. I would tell my parents why after Mass on Sunday. Then I would tell Eric.

So I went to Sunday Mass and took my last Communion at St. Anthony's. I prayed as devoutly as I ever have that God would understand that I still believed in him, that Christ would grant me his charity and love. I felt at peace for the first time in many weeks.

When we reached my parents' home after church, we had our traditional Sunday supper: a beef roast, mashed potatoes, and boiled vegetables. I found myself a little nostalgic and realized I was thinking of the meal as a Last Supper of sorts. Nutritionally I was better off, but the ritual of the meal was as much a part of me as Sunday Communion.

The meal was unexpectedly peaceful. Meg and David had wrought changes in my parents, who seemed more relaxed than I had seen them in a long time. David brought out a maternal playfulness I had never seen in my mother, and I wondered what had made her seem so cold and strict to me. I began to hope that this new mellowness might help them accept what I had to tell them.

After supper my father turned on a football game, and Meg took David upstairs for a changing. Michael huddled in a chair where he could glance at the game, but otherwise occupied himself with his murder mystery. I searched for a way to open the subject and realized there was not going to be an easy way. My palms started to sweat.

My mother, freed from rocking her grandson, said, "Now, Faith Catherine, perhaps you'll tell me why you've been going to some other church for services."

My heart sank. Without David on her lap, she reverted to her usual critical form. "I told you on the phone about last Sunday, Mom," I said, ignoring the three Sundays I hadn't gone at all. "A friend of mine died and it was his funeral service."

"Was he Catholic?"

"No, but it was a Christian service." I saw how I might use this topic to lead in to what I wanted to say. What I'd eaten for supper was sitting in my stomach like a stone.

My mother pursed her lips and asked, "What friend was this?"

"A friend from the university. He and I worked together for several years. He had cancer."

My mother looked at me suspiciously. "He was just a friend?"

The question exasperated me. "Mother, when are you going to stop suspecting me of having affairs?"

"It's my duty to worry about you," she said coldly.

Her duty. Never that she cared about me. I couldn't help but compare her cold duty to the supportive love Sydney had from Carrie, or that Nara had shown me. I remembered suddenly how Carrie had told Sydney she could bring any special person home, no matter who. I hadn't understood then what Carrie had been trying to say: Sydney could bring a woman home with her and her lover would be welcomed.

I envied Sydney from the bottom of my heart. Taking a deep breath, I said, "We were not having an affair. Besides, I found out at the funeral that he was gay."

My father looked up from his football game. "And you stayed?"

"He was a friend, Dad. A good and kind friend."

"You should have left. I thought I taught you better than that."

My mother pressed her hand to her heart. "What if someone who knew your father had seen you there? Your father is the head usher at St. Anthony's Cathedral. There are people who can't wait to spread malicious gossip."

"I can't worry about that," I said, my voice on the edge of shaking.

Michael gave me an odd look and shifted uncomfortably.

My father set his recliner forward. My courage faltered for a moment as I recognized he was prepared to leap to his feet and tower over me, perhaps do worse. "I have to watch my reputation," my father said.

I won't be intimidated, I told myself. The cup is before me and I must drink. "I can't spend my entire life worrying about your reputation, father. I have to —"

He came to his feet and stood in the center of the room. "I won't have my daughter consorting with faggots."

"I am not consorting —" I began in a shaking voice, then stopped. I realized that I had indeed been consorting and would probably happily do so again. I stood up and faced him. "I think you'll have to get used to it."

I gulped at the frozen mask of outrage on his face. My mother gasped.

"I am a lesbian," I said, and then I lifted my chin. Childish, perhaps, but I imagined I was Eleanor facing one of those greedy, prissy abbés who had dared to tell her what she could and could not do. "For obvious reasons I will not be attending Mass in the future."

Michael was staring at me. My father's face was turning purple as he struggled for words.

My mother said in a stunned voice, "You don't know what you're saying."

"I know what I'm saying, and it's not easy to say it. But I won't live a lie."

My father was trembling with anger. I stood my ground as he advanced on me. I couldn't count on Michael's intervention. He might be as angry and repulsed as my father was.

"Unnatural child! I should have had a half-dozen grandchildren by now, but instead you live under my roof and practice your filthy, perverted sins." He spat as he talked, and I could smell his after-dinner whiskey on his breath.

"If you don't want me under your roof again, fine," I said. I stared at him, then at my mother who wouldn't meet my gaze, and finally at Michael.

"Get out of this house, harlot. Get out of my sight until you repent and have done your penance."

I continued to look at Michael who, incredibly, gave me a ghost of a smile. I felt a wave of relief. I no longer cared about my parents, but losing Michael would have been a difficult blow.

"Don't look to your brother for support, tramp. The only thing worse than you would be if my son was a faggot."

"Don't you ever use that word again," Michael said in a voice that silenced the room. Only the roar of the football game continued.

I gaped at him.

My father's attention abruptly diverted from me to Michael. "Are you one too? Are you a faggot?"

Michael got up, a painful process for him, but once on his feet his back was ramrod straight. He looked like the aval officer he was. "I told you not to use that word. You don't even understand what you're saying. If it weren't for a faggot, you wouldn't have a son."

Michael pulled the collar of his shirt down for a moment, making his burn scars painfully visible. "Every night I thank God I'm alive. I'm alive because a faggot pulled me out of that burning room. I've only got burns on my arms and chest. He burned his face. I was lying on my back thinking I'm going to burn to death, and there he was, pulling me out. I saw that faggot's eyebrows catch fire. Do you have any idea what I owe him? He could have left me there, but he kept saying, I've got you, Lieutenant, I've got you. And I'm screaming because I'm on fire, and now he's on fire, and at the same time I'm thinking about how every day someone would write *faggot* on his locker in chalk, and every day he'd have to wipe it off. And I never put a stop to it because of the crap you taught me. Even though I was his lieutenant and he was a damned fine sailor. I never asked, and he never told. And that faggot would have had every right to have left me there to die. But he didn't. So don't you say faggot. I owe my life to a faggot. If they were all like him, I'd want a Navy full of faggots!"

My father's face had gone white, and he suddenly looked older. I thought irrelevantly that the old dog had finally met a young dog he had to bow to. I

174

didn't see his face flush with purple again, and only when Michael lunged forward did I realize my father was swinging back to me.

I had enough time to throw up my hands, then his closed fist slammed into my hands, driving them back into my face so hard I fell across the chair I'd vacated. In another second I was on the floor. Through my ringing ears I heard my father screaming with rage.

My mother didn't move. When I focused my eyes on her I realized she was in a daze, seeing nothing, remembering nothing. She was always that way when he hit me.

I got groggily to my feet and realized that my father had stormed out of the house. Michael steadied me, then slipped his arm around my shoulder.

Meg stood in the door to the hallway holding David, her mouth open and eyes like dinner plates. "Faith, are you all right?"

"I'll live," I said, shakily. I could feel my lower lip swelling, but the skin wasn't broken. He was never going to get another chance to hit me. "You'll be coming to visit me if you want to see me in the future, Meg. I won't come here again."

"What is it?" She stepped warily into the room, looking at my mother for guidance. "Mama, what happened?"

My mother slowly looked up, then seemed to focus on David. Without looking at me, indeed carefully not looking at me, she said to Meg, "You are my only daughter."

"Faith," Meg said. "What the hell did you do? Marry a Jew by chance?" Of all things, she smiled at me.

I realized then that Meg had been where I was now, though my father hadn't ever hit her. I was certainly a late learner. "No," I said, and I managed a weak smile. "But I'll probably marry a woman someday."

Meg shrugged. "Like I didn't know that," she said ironically. "I wondered when you were going to figure it out."

I blinked at her in surprise. "How did you —"

"Abe's sister is gay. He asked me once if you were, and though I said no, it got me thinking. You're lovely to look at and there haven't been many men in your life. There were a couple of guys at church today who made me look twice, but you never look."

"Dad's going to come back soon, Faith. I don't know what he'll do," Michael said. "Spare yourself some grief. I'll come visit."

"I have a sofa if you ever need it," I said. I took a deep breath and turned to my mother. "Good-bye, Mom."

She didn't answer.

"I know you think that God is going to punish me," I said in a flash of anger, "but he's your God, and they're your rules. *You* burn in hell." As soon as I said it, I regretted it. I had been trying to take a higher road than that. Still, I felt better for saying it. My mother just turned her head away.

I picked up my handbag at the door. Meg asked David to give me a kiss, which he did quite willingly. The wet smear was comforting. "Thanks, Meg," I said with a tremulous smile. "Aunt Faith can still babysit."

"I know," she said. She kissed me gently on the

side of my face that was a solid, throbbing ache. "There, all better. Moms have magic kisses, you know." She swallowed and her jaw tightened. "If he ever lays a hand on David I'll kill him."

"They're going to be all alone at the end, you know."

"No," Meg said. "They'll have the Church." She hugged David. "Maybe they're happy with it, but I'd rather have my son."

I reached home in a state of exhaustion and fell asleep with an ice pack on my face. I was roused well after dark by the phone ringing and let my new answering machine take the call.

"Hi there, sweetie. I hope grading your papers is going well. Let's get together this week as soon as you're done, okay? I'm leaving for Hong Kong again next week, so how about Wednesday? And Saturday? I think I can scare up some tickets to a play."

I drowned out the rest of Eric's message by burrowing my head under the sofa cushions. I needed to recover from today's confrontation before I saw Eric, but perhaps Wednesday would be best.

I felt really strange and different, but I didn't feel as awful as I had thought I would. James had been right. I'd lost my parents and was surviving. I'd unexpectedly gained a closer relationship with my brother and sister. And, most unexpectedly of all, I'd gained a better relationship with myself.

9

That which is crooked cannot be made straight.

— ECCLESIASTES 1:15

"Really, Alan? You wouldn't lie to me about a thing like this, would you?" Sydney knew Alan wouldn't, but she wasn't sure she had heard him right.

"You've got the go-ahead to put your name in. Mark says he can almost guarantee no opposition, and perhaps even staunch party support, even though you have those two strikes against you."

"Two strikes? My sexuality and what else?"

Alan laughed. "You're a woman, Sydney, remember?"

"Oh yeah," she said sheepishly. "Sometimes I forget. Well, I don't need any guarantees from Mark, I'll make them on my own." She was tired after nearly two weeks of nonstop work. It was proving good therapy to get past any drinking urges, and she only thought of Faith in the moments before she fell into exhausted sleep each night.

"Well, we'll let Mark live with his fantasy, if you don't mind. At least for now," Alan said, always pragmatic. "Let's get together tomorrow and talk about announcement strategy and staff we'll need to hire. I know at least one speech writer who's eager to come aboard your campaign. After all the money you've given to Emily's List you should get a few personal endorsements there."

"Tomorrow's fine," Sydney said. "I'll clear the evening."

She hung up in a daze and looked around her desk at the case folders. She was going to have to turn many of them over to associates if she wanted time to plan a campaign. The associates would probably be happy, but for a moment Sydney felt a little panic. Her cases, by their sheer number, were steady, grounding, and absorbing. The campaign would be a roller-coaster ride.

She put aside the panic and let the glee of the roller coaster take over. Maybe she wouldn't win, but she would definitely get to say her piece about a lot of issues. Writing discussion briefs and white papers on health-care access, civil rights, domestic violence, education — she looked forward to the challenge.

Would the challenge be enough fulfillment to make her forget about Faith? It had to be, she told herself. In fact, she was quite sure it was.

* * * * *

"I'm so glad to see you," Eric said. He swept me into his arms for a hearty hug, then set me down. As always I felt an inner warmth when he held me, but I no longer considered it something a life partnership could be built on. "Get your coat, it's hellish out there." The warm fall had ended abruptly, and more seasonable rain and cold winds had arrived earlier in the day. "I've got reservations at Ambria, if you feel like French."

"Sure," I said. I couldn't help a nervous swallow. "But can we sit down and talk first? I need to . . . tell you something." My heart started to hammer. I so cared for him and dreaded telling him more than I had dreaded telling my parents. He was going to be hurt, and I would be 100 percent responsible.

"Sure, sweetie." He took off his greatcoat and sat down easily on the sofa, turning toward me as I sat down next to him. He looked so trusting and comfortable. He had no idea what was coming.

"Eric, this is not going to be easy."

He sat forward. "What is it, Faith? Have I offended you?" He suddenly looked like a hurt little boy. "Are you breaking up with me?"

I couldn't speak, so I nodded.

"I thought we got along really well," he said, looking down. I could see he was biting his lower lip.

"We do," I said huskily. "That's why this is so hard and it took me so long."

"Can you give me a reason?"

"Yes. Let me ask you a question, though, because I'm curious." He nodded without looking up. "Why haven't you made any sexual overtures to me?"

His head shot up. "Is that what this about? Are you afraid I'm not really attracted to you? More than anything I respect you, Faith. I could tell you weren't ready for sex, and I was happy to leave it that way. I'm not one of those men who has to have it or die. I frankly don't understand men who can't keep their pants zipped. And we were becoming close friends, and from there I thought, well, I thought we would have something like my parents have. Something that would last forever. I thought sex would come naturally to us when the time was right. I've had some really disastrous relationships that were built on sex, and now friendship matters more to me."

"You are such a rare man," I said. I took his hand. "If I could be with any man, it would be you, Eric. I do love you." I broke off as his fingers tightened on mine. "I've done a lot of soul-searching this last month or two. And I've come to accept the truth about myself. I . . . I'm gay, Eric. I thought I could change myself. I prayed I would change. You don't know how much."

His fingers clenched on mine, then he abruptly let go. He turned his head away, and I saw him take a deep, shuddering breath.

"Eric, I'm so, so sorry. I should never have kept going out with you. I never meant to hurt you." I wiped away a tear. I had done more crying in the last two months than in my entire life. I was sick of being sodden all the time.

"For a minute, I thought you were going to tell me you wanted to be a nun," he said in a low voice. He looked up with a slight smile, but there were tears in his eyes. "Somehow I knew you were too good to be true."

181

"Don't," I said. "I'm not good at all." I mopped ineffectively at my face with an edge of my sleeve, then smiled as he proffered his handkerchief. Always a gentleman, I thought. "You don't know the half of it."

"You don't have to tell me. Faith, sweetie," he said, taking my hand back, "I'd like to stay friends. I mean it."

"I do, too. I wish I could be different."

"As the song goes, I love you just the way you are." He swallowed noisily, then tried for a brave smile with partial success. "I think you've read so much about Eleanor that you're starting to be like her."

"How so?" I blinked at him. If anything, I had compared Eleanor to Sydney in my mind. They were both fearless and ambitious.

"You might have played it safe, but instead you've chosen to sail off to the unknown." He sighed.

"I don't feel like I chose anything," I said slowly. "I just stopped denying the inevitable."

He patted my hand and gave me a resigned look. "This may seem anticlimactic but I'm starving, and I really could use the company of a good friend since my girlfriend just dumped me." I smiled at him with a sniffle. "Why don't you get your coat, okay?"

In a misty daze, feeling far better than I thought I would, I let him help me on with my coat. He turned me to face him and buttoned me up as if I were a little girl. "It's cold out — sweetie, what happened to your face?"

I realized then that my mopping with his handkerchief had disturbed the careful layer of makeup I'd used to hide the yellowing bruise. "It's not important."

"Somebody hit you," he said in disbelief. "Were you mugged?"

"Eric, it doesn't matter, and it won't happen again. I won't be going home again. Let's just say that my father wasn't as reasonable as you were."

"Jesus Christ," he said. "Your father hit you? You said he was very religious."

It was my turn to sigh. "So was Pope Alexander the sixth, and he poisoned people, or had his daughter Lucretia Borgia to do it."

"Jesus Christ," he said again. Shocked to the core, he gently touched the side of my face. "I can't believe this. Sydney came to a family weekend with a woman, and both of them were roaring drunk. They were crawling all over each other. My parents hadn't known until then that she was a lesbian, and I thought my father would have a stroke. He was so angry with her, but never, ever would he have hit her. I just . . . I can't believe that people hit their kids."

"Sometimes I think you are the most innocent person I've ever met," I said. "Let's not talk about it, okay? It's over and I'm done with it."

I could see it cost him an effort to let the matter drop. "Are you trying to tell me that I'm Louis to your Eleanor?"

"Silly," I said, affectionately. "You are not a naive and pious monk. And I'm not a brave, adventurous queen."

"Hmmm," he said as he opened the door. "If I'm Louis and you're Eleanor, then someday I'll look forward to seeing who your Henry is."

"Henrietta," I said, trying to make him smile. I thought abruptly of Renee. I knew that she would gloat when she found out she'd been right about me. No matter, let her gloat. She would never be my Henry.

As I locked the door I told myself I'd already met my Henry. She'd kissed me in a field of gold. But I was no Eleanor of Aquitaine. I'd left my home far enough behind. I needed to feel reconnected with my classes. I wanted to call Nara and cement what seemed like a promising friendship. I would be happy to stay in one place mentally for quite a while.

"Syd, that was possibly the greatest speech of your career! We're off to a *fabuloso* start!"

Sydney returned Carmen's hug and said with a laugh, "I practiced on the plane."

Carmen propelled Sydney from the head table and through the milling crowds leaving the opening luncheon of the National Conference on Homelessness. "I expected you to give the implementation of Measure D, but you also gave us a snapshot of the entire federal funding picture. And your slides were great. You've given people something to focus on in the roundtables."

Sydney was feeling a little high. She'd worked hard on the speech, and the result was worth it. Carmen, the other cochair, was one of the most brutally honest people Sydney knew. If Carmen said it was good, then it must have been.

She spent the afternoon in roundtables and then shook about five hundred hands at the reception. She discovered that the rumors of her running for the Illinois State Senate had surfaced, probably spread by the other Chicagoans present, because many of the women commented on it and wished her well.

After the reception, she took leave of everyone and walked briskly down Market Street. She wasn't staying in the main conference hotel because she wanted to avoid the inevitable friendly groups that gathered in the bar. She was capable of having club soda and enjoying herself for a while, but being in another hotel made it easier to leave early. Besides, she had another speech in the morning and wanted to run through it one more time before doing a little sightseeing on her own.

The Palace Hotel had a lovely old-world feel and was only two blocks away. It sat at the nexus of most of the city's mass transit, was in the heart of the business district, and was only a stone's throw from the Museum of Modern Art. Sydney thought she'd see the museum tomorrow during the one break in her schedule. Tonight she wanted to visit the Castro District. She'd been there before but hadn't been sober, and as a result she didn't remember much.

Fog was rapidly settling on the city, and Sydney hastened her pace. It felt almost like rain, but the sky had been beautifully clear all day. She skirted the subway steps and nearly fell over a woman and toddler huddled together under a dirty blanket.

"I'm sorry," Sydney said. She reached into her handbag and gave the woman a twenty. Without a word the woman scooped up the child and blanket and hurried down into the subway. What a life, Sydney thought. Half the people at the conference would have said Sydney had done the wrong thing. Handouts didn't solve homelessness and only encouraged the government to expect individuals to help. True, she thought as she looked at the retreating woman and child. But promises of social service programs wouldn't feed the little one tonight. She would never miss the twenty dollars.

She started to turn back toward the hotel when a woman coming up the subway steps caught her eye. No, she thought. I'm just wistful, that's all. Still, she couldn't look away. To her intense frustration, seeing someone who looked a little like Faith happened weekly and every time it happened she was no more able to look away than she was now.

Except now she wasn't just imagining and hoping. Now she was sure. It was Faith. Damnation! She'd forgotten that Faith would be in San Francisco as well. But why should she have worried about it? The city was enormous. How could they be in the same place at the same time?

She told herself to duck into the hotel, but she remained rooted to the spot regardless of the harried commuters who were pushing against her. She willed Faith to look up. And then she did.

Her face was as cool and serene as Sydney had ever had seen it for one moment, then a flame seemed to erupt from within and Faith's eyes glowed. When she reached the top step she stood looking at

Sydney, and Sydney gazed back, as if she had crossed a desert and Faith was the oasis.

"Eric's favorite hotel," Faith said. "But the conference isn't here. I checked. I . . . I didn't do this deliberately."

"The thought never crossed my mind," Sydney said in a low voice.

"You told me to stay away. I did." A surge of commuters jostled Faith, and Sydney realized that talking in the misting fog in the middle of rush hour was not exactly productive.

"I know," she said, reaching to take Faith's arm. She pulled gently, and Faith followed without demur. She led Faith up the hotel steps and into the gleaming teak and brass bar just inside the door.

They settled into a booth across from each other. Faith said nothing, just continued to look at Sydney, her green eyes glowing with something almost fierce.

"Don't look at me like that," Sydney said, crossly.

"Like what?"

Sydney looked down at her hands. She should leave. Seeing Faith was exactly the wrong thing to do. A waiter hovered at her elbow. Distracted, she said, "Club soda."

Faith ordered a club soda as well. "You didn't order two fingers of Glen," she said with a little smile.

At least that much of her self-defense was working, Sydney thought. Five minutes ago I was all put together, ready to slay my dragons and conquer the world. "I'm not upset." I'm a fucking basket case, that's what I am.

Faith frowned, looking puzzled. "I didn't think you were."

"Look at me," Sydney said, holding up her trembling hands. "Jesus, Faith. Why are you doing this to me?"

"I'm not doing anything," Faith said, her tone going sharp. "You brought me in here. I'd be quite happy in my room looking over my notes from today."

"Fine by me," Sydney said. Better to show Faith anger than the emotion roiling around inside of her that she wasn't willing to name.

Faith pressed her lips together and started to slide out of the booth.

"Faith, don't go. I'm being a bitch." I can't do it, Sydney thought. I can't send her away. She smiled as charmingly as she could manage. "Forgive me."

There was a long silence after Faith settled in again and the waiter brought their drinks. Then Faith said, "Have you talked to Eric lately?"

"No," Sydney said. "He's in New York, isn't he?"

Faith nodded. "I broke up with him, Sydney. He was upset, but not devastated."

"I'm glad you told him," Sydney said. She'd avoided talking to Eric because she knew the topic of Faith would come up, and she didn't want to find herself in a position where lying was the only way not to reveal what she already knew. Eric could put two and two together as well as anyone.

Faith sipped her club soda, looking as if it was just a way to pass the time. Sydney watched a drop run down the side of her glass. It merged with another, then split again. No distractions. A life that can bear examining. If she wanted to be an Illinois state senator she couldn't give the media anything to gossip about, like a new girlfriend. Especially one who until recently had been dating her brother. Getting involved with Faith would mean putting off running for office, perhaps indefinitely.

"Have dinner with me," Sydney said. She felt as if she was watching a play with herself as the lead character, and she had no idea what her next line would be, and no idea if it was a comedy or tragedy. "I was going to go to the Castro district. Every time my aide, John, comes to San Francisco he goes to this restaurant he says is fabulous."

Faith was nodding, her eyes looking glassy. "I'll meet you back at the main door in fifteen minutes or so."

Sydney nodded and watched Faith leave. She realized she was alone in a bar for the first time in a long, long time. But she felt no temptation. The most tempting thing in her life had just walked out the door.

She really had been able to put Faith away in her mind. But it was just like in the first days when she had been sober. She was fine until she saw a bottle of Scotch or smelled alcohol, and then the longing would come back so strong she'd give in. She had lived the first seven days of sobriety over three times. After the weekend at her parents' she'd thought of Faith hourly. Then daily, and then weekly. But it had taken two seconds in Faith's presence to undo all the forgetting.

She couldn't twelve-step her feelings for Faith, nor could she hide away from temptation like she had from alcohol. She couldn't retreat to a remote cabin and read for months. If they ran into each other two thousand miles from home, what would it be like when they inevitably ran into each other in Chicago?

She knew that Faith believed in God in a far more personal way than Sydney did. Sydney was skeptical enough not to believe in divine intervention. This was just a stupid coincidence because they had both taken Eric's advice about where to stay. But the chance encounter had shaken the Ice Queen to her very foundations.

She muttered to herself all the way back to her room. Why had she asked Faith out? She couldn't do this. Alan Stevens would kill her. Mark O'Leary would kill her. John, who wanted very badly to be a senator's aide, would kill her.

Men. What did they know about that incredible light in Faith's eyes when she looked at Sydney? They would never know that the light promised passion like nothing Sydney had never experienced before. In the elevator she shuddered, remembering Faith's wetness and urgency and the silk of her skin against Sydney's fingers. Alan, Mark, and John — none of them would understand it. Alan and Mark would most likely think Faith had a nice caboose and leave it at that. John never noticed women unless they had power.

She unlocked her door and told herself that none of them would be able to resist the very thing that made them feel whole and alive, nor would they expect it of one another. Why was she the one who had to just say no?

Dry up, she scolded herself. You once believed that alcohol made you whole and kept you alive.

Faith is nothing more than another addiction, she told herself sternly.

She looked at herself in the mirror. My name is Sydney, and I'm a Faith-a-holic. She sighed heavily. That was not going to work.

Sydney was watching me from the moment I left the elevator. I'd dressed sensibly in slacks and a sweater and carried a rain jacket. I hadn't believed Eric when he said that it rained fog in San Francisco, but he'd been right.

She had changed into slacks as well, and wore an elegant suede bomber-style jacket over a close-fitting white button-up shirt. Like her John Adams costume, the effect had masculine overtones, but there would never be any doubt in anyone's mind that Sydney was a woman.

I had promised myself not to say a word to her about how I felt or how she made me feel. She didn't want me to, she said, though at times what she said and how she looked at me were two different things. Sometimes what she said was conflicting. Still, I would say nothing. But I could look all I wanted.

"The doorman assures me a cab is fastest, even though the subway goes right there," Sydney said.

"Whatever you say," I said, and off we went in a cab. The driver seemed intent on breaking speed records, and if I didn't look at the other cars I was only half terrified.

We were briskly deposited in front of a restaurant called Ma Tante Sumi. Looking up and down the quiet, fog-shrouded street, I was struck by how much this street was like any other. Passersby appeared to be on their way home from work. From the way my father and *The Gay Agenda* had carried on, I had expected half-naked women and men in dresses on every corner.

The restaurant was small, and the cuisine a combination of Japanese, French, and Vietnamese. Each course had two choices, and in the pleasure of the excellent food I found myself relaxing.

"The tapestries are in excellent condition," I told her after she asked. "I'm pretty sure that they are copies of paintings that copied original tapestries, and faithful reproductions at that. The Christian motifs woven into the borders are faithful to other art from the time of the Second Crusade, but there are some esoteric cabalistic mystical symbols as well. The paintings were probably done in the high French Renaissance when they didn't mind risking censure for duplicating the symbols. The tapestries I'm looking at were done in the early seventeen hundreds on a British royal commission. Whichever of the Williams it was would not have asked to have those symbols added, so they must have already been there in the original tapestries."

"And what does that tell you?" Sydney looked interested and a little amused.

I felt sheepish and realized I'd been running on. "I left out the point, didn't I? Well, the motifs in the borders are themselves overtly Christian. But the cabalistic symbols are Jewish in origin. I'm going to ask a Hebrew scholar I know what they are, but I think I know already. One at least represents the belief that the messiah is yet to come."

"Oh," Sydney said. "Sort of the whole point of the Crusades. So whoever wove the original tapestries was making a bit of a statement, weren't they?"

I grinned. "A twelfth-century joke."

"Are you finding them inspiring to look at?"

"Indeed," I said. "The idea that eight hundred years later I can look at something that Eleanor saw — granted she had originals and I have copies — is thrilling. I suddenly realized she must have had a wild sense of humor. She was very intelligent, and I'm sure she recognized the symbols for what they were. She probably enjoyed laughing at her critics because they didn't understand the joke. I feel kinship because I am laughing with her."

I savored my salmon filet with creamed pumpkin sauce. It was incredibly subtle in flavor, and I offered Sydney a bite in return for a sample of her squab with roasted pepper sauce. Before I knew it, we were enjoying decadent desserts, Sydney having convinced them to leave the dark cherry sauce off the chocolate torte, and then Sydney was paying the bill. It was as if no time had passed at all. We'd been so comfortable together it reminded me of how pleasant dining with Eric had always been.

We bundled into our jackets and stepped out into the misty evening. By Chicago standards it was brisk, but I saw people in hats and gloves who looked pinched and miserable.

"Want to see the Castro?" Sydney asked as we stood at the curb.

I glanced around. The fog had blanketed the street, and everything was very quiet. "Isn't this it?"

"We're on the edge," she said. She led the way, and as we walked downhill several blocks the traffic in the streets and on the sidewalks increased until we reached a corner of Castro Street itself. The street was so busy and brightly lit that the fog receded and it was possible to see for a block in either direction.

What struck me first was not the men in leather and the women holding hands, but the mix of races. Chicago is a divided place. Each neighborhood has its own makeup, and the only real mixing takes place in the downtown district on the job. As I stood there I could see the full array of human ethnicity and race as well as a rainbow of hair colors and dress styles. The only real division was between the genders. Groups were made up almost exclusively of either men or women. And generally, everyone was laughing and obviously having a good time.

We ducked into a bookstore and Sydney bought several novels while I browsed. Then we wandered into a hardware store of all things, and I bought a small rainbow-striped troll that reminded me for some reason of James. I wondered what he would have said if he'd known where I was, walking around in a place where people felt so free to hold hands, kiss, and flirt.

It wasn't until we walked past a bar where men could sit and watch the street that I felt uncomfortable. Even though their ready-for-sex stares weren't aimed at me, it still seemed predatory. But then again the bar in the hotel had predators, too, and they *had* been staring at me. Then I saw a man in chaps with most of his behind exposed. I told myself that freedom was freedom and left it at that. Still, it reminded me of *The Gay Agenda*.

As we passed a movie theater showing something

called *Seduction: The Cruel Woman,* I saw women in leather. I'd never seen anything like them before — leather pants, hats, vests, some with metal studs, and high boots all in black. The outfits were all slightly different, but from the same theme, like knights with different shields. I smiled to myself as I realized my father would have had a heart attack if he saw them or knew I was looking and admiring.

I saw an older woman with gray hair cut in a pageboy holding a leash that was attached to a much younger blonde with elaborate makeup and teased hair. The blonde was wearing spiked heels so high she was on tiptoe. Her leather pants were so tight I could see the outline of her genitalia. She kept her eyes on the ground and only moved forward when the older woman pulled on the leash.

The older woman saw me staring and curled her lip, then boldly rubbed her crotch. She sneered when I blanched. I looked around wildly for Sydney and realized she hadn't seen me stop. I hurried up the street after her.

My stomach was churning, and I realized that I had harbored a secret hope that the video footage in *The Gay Agenda* had been faked. Especially the scene where two women in leather were demonstrating how to tie up a woman. The scene had ended as one of them picked up a whip, and it had truly horrified me. I could intellectually deal with all the other images, but that one had stayed with me. I hadn't wanted to believe that women did that to each other. But why would women be different from men when it comes to the full range of sexual expression? I knew I was being prudish, but it was a lot for me to absorb all at once.

Sydney had stopped to gaze into a shop window. I was lost in thought until she asked me what I thought of a vase.

I took so long to answer that she shook my arm gently.

"What's wrong, Faith?"

"Did you see that young girl on a leash? I really didn't believe women did that. I thought they made it up. I don't know what to think," I babbled. "It's their lives, but it's ... I mean, it does make me uncomfortable. It's just that, well, do you approve?"

"It's not for me to approve or disapprove," Sydney said carefully.

"Don't be a politician," I said with a snap. I was troubled and needed to know what she thought.

"I mean it. It's not my idea of a relationship or sex. But I cannot say I disapprove because it's only a stone's throw from my disapproving of their lifestyle to how most people disapprove of mine."

"But it's not the same thing at all," I stuttered.

"It's about the freedom to enjoy sex — consenting sex — between adults. A part of gay rights is sexual freedom. Without it we'll never have social freedom. But I have to be honest. There's a fine line between some sex and violence, and I do wonder what is healthy and what isn't. I have to accept that I'm not the one to draw the line for anyone but myself."

I looked over her shoulder at my reflection in the shop window. "I don't want people to think that's the way I live."

Sydney half smiled. "I know what you mean. I get really testy when people assume that being a lesbian is only about sex. And that lesbians must think about sex all the time. And that all lesbians wear leather and are sado-masochists." She shrugged. "Sometimes people can get past the stereotypes and sometimes they can't."

"Am I being silly?" I thought of the years I'd wasted in a closet I wouldn't even name because of stereotypes.

"Well," Sydney said, "look around you. How many women on leashes do you see?"

I frowned. "None of course."

"But believe me, if the radical right brought cameras through here, they'd have five minutes of footage of that one woman on a leash and five seconds of the other hundreds of women who are not on leashes."

"Like in *The Gay Agenda*," I said. "Have you seen it?"

She hissed. "I was so angry I nearly threw up. It's so incredibly wrong. But they keep updating it and sending it out, and I swear half the footage isn't even necessarily gay people. S and M is not exclusively a homosexual practice. Heterosexuals do it too and no one films it as a part of a heterosexual agenda." Her eyes blazed with indignation. "When a local talk show featured clips from it, my mother called me and said how angry it had made her because they made it sound like their footage of the most outrageous and flamboyant gay people they could find was representative of all of us. Most people are smart enough to see through that kind of lie, and those that aren't, well, they won't vote for me anyway."

I managed a laugh. "My parents are definitely not smart enough. If I hadn't already left, they'd have kicked me out." I couldn't tell her my father had hit me, not because I was ashamed of it, but because I didn't want to upset her on my behalf. "I went to a Dignity support group meeting and I'm not alone in being exiled from both family and church. But my brother and sister are still talking to me."

"I'm glad for that," Sydney said. She patted my arm, then let her hand run down it until she could twine her fingers with mine. "I was really crude when I came out to my parents. I didn't so much come out as fall down on another woman at a family gathering. They forgave me, something I can still hardly believe."

"Your parents are darlings," I said enviously. I took a deep breath and nodded toward the window. "That vase is very pretty."

Sydney let go of my hand and said, "I've got nowhere to put it. Oh well."

We continued window shopping down Market Street for a block or so. The pedestrians were just like those in a Chicago suburb, except that most couples were same sex. I began to recover my sense of the simple freedom of all types of people happily going about their lives without glancing over their shoulder. Even though the woman on the leash had shocked me, I wasn't going to let it overshadow the rest of what I saw: everyday people doing everyday kinds of things. Two women with their arms around each other's waist emerged from a Mexican restaurant completely at ease with each other. I wondered if I'd ever reach that stage.

I asked Sydney something I'd been wondering about. "Do a lot of people want to talk about your sex life? I mean, when you ran for office before?"

"They wanted to, but since there's nothing to talk about it's a rather short subject."

"Is that what it takes? Do you have to be celibate if you're gay and want to hold public office?"

Sydney stopped walking and looked at me. "I hadn't really thought about it globally. For me, well, now that I think about it, the other gay politicians I know do share a sense of higher burden. Our opponents are ready to jump on anything no matter how innocent and accuse us of sexual aberrations. Just about everyone I can think of is either in a highly visible monogamous long-term relationship or completely without rumor of any relationship. There are probably exceptions. Of course that doesn't include the people in the closet. It isn't fair, but that's the way it is."

I read between the lines. She was as much as telling me that we really did have no future, whether Eric was in the picture or not. Eric was out of the picture as far as I was concerned, but Sydney could very well not want to hurt him further by being with the woman he might have been falling in love with. She owed him so much. Sydney's gratitude to her brother plus her political ambitions equaled no relationship with me.

The sooner I left her company, the better. There was a new pain inside me, and being with her was only making it worse.

"I'm getting a little tired," I said. "If you want to stay I can take a cab back. Or the subway. It's right up the street."

"I've got a speech to review," she said, looking serious. "Let's call it a night."

As we turned toward the subway I thought we

weren't just calling it a night. We were calling it quits. Whatever hopes I had cherished that our chance meeting would undo the past were gone. And I would pay for my night in her company by having to say good-bye again.

10

Strength and honor are her clothing.

— PROVERBS 31:25

There were no cabs in sight and we were almost to the subway when a woman coming out of a coffee-house exclaimed, "Sydney! I didn't know you'd be out and about tonight. We could have had dinner or something."

We stopped. The other woman, about my age with large, sparkling eyes, must have realized that Sydney wasn't alone. She seemed taken aback, then looked pointedly at Sydney and inclined her head toward me.

"Angie, this is Faith Fitzgerald, a friend from

home. We ran into each other at my hotel. Faith, this is Angela Davis Washington."

It was obvious that Angie didn't think it was a surprise at all. "You look familiar," she said. "I know. You and Syd were at Liz's. A couple of months ago."

"Another coincidence," Sydney said.

"Really," I added, wondering why the point was so important to Sydney. I remembered Angie now. We hadn't been introduced, but she'd been wearing a stunning dashiki that had caught my eye.

"Secret's safe with me," Angie said. "Where are you headed?"

"I have a speech to work on," Sydney said. "So it's back to the hotel for me. How about you, Faith?"

"I need to review my notes," I said. We took our leave just as several other women joined Angie, some calling out to Sydney that they'd see her tomorrow.

"Damn," Sydney was muttering under her breath.

"What's wrong?"

"Angie's a delegate to the party convention. She's never going to believe that we're not having an affair. A big part of my strategy is my image. Angie isn't going to tarnish me, but she's sure to mention that I appear to have a girlfriend at long last. As everyone knows, a lesbian with a girlfriend means kinky, scandalous sex. From there it's just a stone's throw to rumors of orgies and blood sacrifices."

"How ridiculous," I said. I was hard pressed to keep up with her rapid stride. "It isn't true."

"Truth hardly matters in politics," she said sulkily, then snapped her hand up to catch the attention of a passing cab.

"I'm surprised you sully yourself with it," I said dryly, but she didn't hear me as she got into the cab.

We rode back to the hotel in silence. The city seemed quiet under the blanket of fog. The buildings had soft corners, and the streetlights were surrounded by iridescent halos.

I didn't know what I had expected from the evening, but it had certainly gone places I hadn't anticipated. I knew I didn't want it to be over, but I couldn't think of a way to prolong it. I didn't want to say good-bye even though an instinct for self-preservation told me I had to.

Sydney was definitely brooding about the encounter with Angie. I had the urge to tease her out of her mood, but it was hardly my place to do so. After all, I wasn't her girlfriend. Not even a friend, when it came right down to it.

"Thank you for dinner," I said as we reached the hotel elevator. "It was lovely."

"You're welcome," she said, automatically. "I'm glad you enjoyed it."

We got on the elevator and she pressed 10 after I pressed 12. "Isn't this where I say let's do it again sometime?"

She blinked at me and then smiled a little. "I don't mean to end our evening on a down note. I feel petty. It shouldn't upset me so much."

"I could cheer you up and tell you how nice Eric was when I told him." It was a lame suggestion, but she nodded after a moment's pause. I got off the elevator with her on her floor. She had one of the corner suites with a large sitting room and a sizable table that she was using as her desk.

"May I get you something to drink?" she offered as I took off my coat. She opened the minibar and came up with a Diet Coke. "There's another one of these in here."

"Sure," I said. I don't really like soda very much, but I was to the point where I'd have drunk Drano to stay with her. My ears were ringing; I was starting to feel like I had the night of the costume party. If I had my way, the evening would end with her hands on me, in me. I flushed as I imagined my mouth on her.

Thankfully, she didn't look at me as she sat down in the room's other guest chair. "So how did he take it?" She sipped her soda and studied the carpet.

"He was sweet," I said, then described my talk with Eric as best I could. "And after dinner he gave me this," I said, holding out my right hand.

She took my fingertips in her hand and pulled them under the light. "How unusual," she said, examining the ring Eric had given me. It fit perfectly on my little finger.

"I wasn't going to take it at first, but he told me it was something he'd seen and knew it was meant for me. He seemed genuinely upset when I said I really shouldn't accept it, so I changed my mind. I felt like wearing it when I looked at the tapestries." The ring was a wide gold band, heavily engraved and very old. He admitted it had been expensive, but the way he said it I was certain I didn't want to know how expensive.

"It is very unusual, and he was right. It is very you," she said. "Are those peacocks?" She turned my hand over.

"It's a traditional medieval engraving pattern."

"It does suit you," Sydney said. Her breath whispered over my palm and I controlled a shudder. "He guessed your ring size pretty well. Very perceptive of him. I'm not sure many men could guess accurately."

"Why not?" She didn't let go of my hand, and I certainly wasn't going to pull it away.

"They're not lesbians," she murmured. "Do they stop to think about the size of a woman's fingers? They might notice their overall shape, maybe whether they're tapered or square. But they wouldn't know their individual characters because they don't think about them as . . ." her voice trailed away.

After a full minute of silence, I gently said, "Sydney? Come back."

She looked up slowly. "Faith," she whispered. Her eyes looked feverish. "Help me."

"Tell me how," I said, alarmed. I tried to pull my hand away, but her grip on it tightened.

She looked down at my hand, then slowly brought it to her lips. "I think about your hands, how small they are, but how strong your fingers seem. How you keep your nails short and you don't wear nail polish —"

The brush of her lips on my open palm shot a tingle of electricity through me. "Sydney, what are you doing?"

"And I can imagine how they might feel on me," she said, as if I hadn't spoken. She looked up again, her lips parted. "And in me. I wanted you so much that night. I haven't stopped wanting you."

She kissed my palm, and waves of sensation made me gasp. It was nothing like when Renee had touched me. This was sweeter. I could feel the pulse of Sydney's heartbeat. I felt the pulse in my throat race to match hers.

"How can I help you, Sydney? Tell me what you want."

"I don't know what I want," she said. She kissed my wrist. "I'm in a bad way for you," she said huskily. "I don't think I could say no to anything tonight."

She kissed my palm again, then lightly trailed the tip of her tongue over it. My heart thumped painfully. Amazing that such a simple caress could focus every nerve in my body on such a small patch of skin.

"Take me to bed, Faith." Sydney slowly stood and pulled me up with her. "I won't be able to think until you do. I can't believe I feel like this. I can't help myself."

To my horror, a tear trickled down her cheek. I pulled her close. "Don't, darling, don't."

"I don't want to lose control like this," she muttered into my shoulder. "I promised myself I wouldn't."

"I'll go if you want."

"No," she gasped. "I meant it. Take me to bed." She led me by the hand into the bedroom and began unbuttoning her shirt. When the third button wouldn't come undone, she pulled the shirt over her head. She captured my hands and brought them to her breasts. With a deft motion she unhooked her bra and pulled it away so my hands were stroking her bare flesh.

I was pulled into the whirlpool of her passion. She finished undressing, her movements urgent. She turned away for a moment and threw back the bed-clothes. She pulled me down onto her. My body finally began to move and whatever might have been long frozen in me melted into her need.

"I don't want to be like this," Sydney whispered in my ear.

I whispered back, "Like what?"

"Needing something so much I can't live without it. Please . . . please touch me."

She was already bringing herself against my hip with urgent pressure. I reverently stroked her bare thigh. It had been so long since I'd felt another woman's skin against my fingertips like this. I started to lower my head to kiss her thigh, but she caught me and pulled me to her for a close, deep kiss.

"Hold me," she said. "Hold me while you take me. I need to know it's you."

"It's me, Syd," I said as I slipped my hand between her clenched thighs. "Relax, darling. I want this as much as you do."

"Hurry," she whispered.

This was a side of Sydney I would never have thought existed, a side that intoxicated me. My head swam as she slowly parted her thighs to my seeking fingers. I wished that I'd stopped to take off my clothes, but remembered how Renee had sometimes liked me to be naked while she was dressed. Until this moment I had not understood how powerful it must have made her feel. I certainly felt it, and the emotion brought a new pounding to my already throbbing body.

Sydney moaned, bringing me back to the here and now, her silky wetness on the very tips of my fingers. I realized I had terrible power over her in that moment, and I could have made her do anything. I stroked her slowly, and she gasped.

I wouldn't make her do anything. I would let her tell me, lead me, into giving her what she needed.

"Please, Faith." She looked up at me, her voice barely above a whisper. "I'll beg if you want me to. I'm too far gone to be proud."

"Tell me what you want. I'm out of practice."

"I want to feel you inside me."

"Yes," I whispered. My fingertips were drowning in her wetness. She shuddered and her hands left my shoulders to guide me farther into her.

We were beyond words after that. We moved toward her climax with fevered kisses and murmurs of encouragement. She clutched me to her as she peaked, holding a cry back in her throat until her shaking wrung it out of her in short bursts. I rested my head on her breast, breathing hard and wanting so much to do it all again.

The thought must have crossed her mind because she smiled slightly as she moved her hips, drawing in a long, pleased breath.

"That was rather nice," she said, closing her eyes. "I don't know why I thought it would hurt me."

I raised my head to smile softly at her. "Sex is one of the nine reasons for reincarnation. The other eight are unimportant."

"Henry Miller," she murmured. Her contented smile slowly faded and she opened her eyes. She raised her head to kiss me. "I thought I'd hate having you see me like this."

"How could I hate it?" My hungry gaze swept down her body.

"Because I hate myself when I'm weak," she said. She arched her back and sighed as my fingers began to stroke her again. "It took me a long time to find my backbone."

"This isn't weakness. It takes too much strength to admit what we want. Don't hate it," I said. "Not when I love it so much. You're like touching fire." I couldn't find any words, so I brushed my wet fingers across her breasts, then returned to her soft, eager wetness.

"Yes, again," she murmured. "And then . . . when I catch my breath . . ." She gazed up at me and vertigo swept over me. Her lips were parted and the curve of her mouth was a promise.

She made good her promise, slowly removing my clothes and kissing my trembling skin when it was bared. She understood that my whimpers as she made love to my breasts meant I wanted more.

Her descent was excruciatingly slow. Somehow she knew that was what I wanted, to climb to another, headier level of desire that could only be satisfied by her mouth on me. I found myself begging, and she teased me further. I hadn't thought to ever let another human being see my need again. Renee had used it to satisfy her own first. But Sydney was intent on my pleasure as she flicked her tongue lightly over me. I saw a fierce, joyful expression cross her face when I responded with a shudder of ecstasy.

And then her mouth was on me, and I felt my body rising as the years of denial surged into a single certainty and unshakable self-knowledge. This was what I was, what I wanted. Another woman to make love to me.

As my body writhed in response, her hands gripping me as she used her lips, her tongue, her teeth to bring me to a shattering climax, I knew that I wanted more. I wanted this woman, for always.

I struggled out of the fog of sleep and groped around me for a blanket to cover us. The sheets were on the floor along with most of the pillows.

"Ummm," she said sleepily, shifting her position so her head was no longer on my arm. "I'm starving."

"Me, too, but I'm more cold."

"Let's see what's in the minibar. I think I saw some cheese." She padded into the outer room. I followed after wrapping myself in a sheet.

The light from the small refrigerator illuminated the body I'd worshiped so thoroughly for several hours. She closed the door, but the image remained burned into my retinas.

"Want some of these?" She flipped on the light over the bar and turned to face me with a can of nuts in one hand. She froze, and across the few feet that separated us we shared a moment of complete understanding. She put down the can and sank down into the chair behind her. I let the sheet fall as I took the two steps necessary to reach her, sinking to my knees to taste her again.

We settled down to sleep in the middle of the floor with the sheet wrapped around us. I was too tired to move.

"Enough, Faith?" Sydney nuzzled my ear.

"Ummm," I said sleepily.

"That's not an answer," she said, and one hand began lazily stroking my breast. It was not a noise of protest that escaped my throat when she slipped the same lazy hand between my thighs again.

"Never enough," I whispered, hoping she was too intent on arousing me again to hear me. "I'll never get enough of you."

"Not as good as last night," Carmen said, "but still right on. You seem a little distracted, and I can guess why."

Sydney took note of the smirk on Carmen's face and decided not to ask. "I'm glad that's the last speech for me. I've only got the moderating on to-morrow's panel left."

"Sleep would help," Carmen said, her smirk deepening. "You probably didn't get much."

"Carmen," Sydney protested. "Don't."

"Too soon to tease you? I mean you brought her with you so it must be serious."

"I didn't bring her with me," Sydney protested. "Really. We met by accident." Then she blushed, something she hadn't done for years.

Carmen hooted. "Accident or not, girlfriend, you've finally done the deed. I'm happy for you. Your life was getting a little too pure and righteous. It's nice to know you're human."

"Nice to know I have a weakness," Sydney muttered.

"Oh dry up," Carmen said. "You're full of yourself

sometimes. It's nice to know that you can want the same things the rest of us do."

"Thanks, Carmen," Sydney snapped, then her temper softened. "I mean it. No one tells me the truth anymore. So thanks."

"You're welcome. I'm off to my panel. Get some sleep before you fall down." Carmen disappeared into one of the meeting rooms.

Sydney walked slowly back to her hotel, where she hoped Faith had found the note she'd left saying when she'd return. She stopped for a moment to sit in the sun. She wanted with every inch of her body to go back to Faith. But an affair with Faith would end all her hopes for the senate seat that would let her do so much good.

The sun warmed her and she turned her face up to soak it in. She wanted to be warm. She wanted to feel all the time like she did when she was with Faith. She had thought these heady feelings of completion and joy could come from work. She knew many women who found their life's joy in their work. But Faith made her think she wasn't one of them.

What could she do about it? An affair was not what she wanted. And she had no idea what Faith wanted. Could she offer Faith more than an affair? She had never asked herself if she could have more or even deserved more. The things she'd done when she'd been drinking . . . if Faith only knew.

She let the sun heat her skin and pictured herself ten years, twenty, thirty years in the future. She couldn't really see herself clearly, but bright as day was Faith by her side.

* * * * *

Sometime in the night we had struggled back into the bedroom, and when I finally woke the next morning there was a note from Sydney on the pillow saying the Do Not Disturb sign was on the door. She could get away at eleven and could I please stay or leave her a note about where I would be.

It was already past eleven and I was late for my appointment at the museum. I pulled back a curtain to discover the fog completely gone. The sky was an overwhelming blue for November. Down on Market Street people were sunning themselves on the steps in front of the subway entrance.

I found my purse and the curator's phone number and, feeling a little foolish and guilty, explained that the weather had proved too tempting for me. The curator, a nice older man with an amazing handlebar mustache, urged me to enjoy the day and said he would see me tomorrow.

I definitely felt as if I were playing hooky as I stepped into the shower. I needed to clean up, get back into my clothes, and go to my own room to change.

I was shampooing my hair in the palatial shower — the one in my room was much more utilitarian — when I saw someone moving through the misted glass doors.

"Sydney, is that you?"

"Yes," came the answer. The door opened and she peered in. "Thank you for staying. I hope it wasn't inconvenient."

I shook my head, feeling shy and completely unsure what to do with my hands. I fought the urge to cover my breasts. We'd done incredibly intimate things to each other the night before, but I felt naked for the first time.

"I'm free until three and then I'll be free after six. I'd like to spend the time with you," she said softly.

I rinsed soap off my face and gazed at her. "Are you sure? It could cause talk."

She kicked off her shoes and slipped out of her suit jacket. In another moment her skirt hit the floor. She stepped into the shower still wearing everything else. "Let's give them something to talk about," she said with a wicked smile.

"Sydney, you're getting all wet. Your lovely blouse —"

"I guess you'll have to take it off me," she said.

I struggled with the wet buttons and found she was ticklish. "This would be easier if you would stop your vellication, ma'am."

"I'll wiggle as much as I want," she answered, laughing.

I kissed her throat. "Jackleg. Logroller. Peanut."

"Are you trying to impugn my profession? That's rich coming from a philologaster like you."

"I am *not* a philologaster," I said indignantly. "I take things very seriously. Like this," I said, and I lowered my mouth to her breasts.

Her laughter faded as we discovered each other again. It was less intense than the night before, but all the more pleasurable to me because I knew that we could build a lifetime on these simple caresses and relaxed, shared intimacy. Expecting every time to be like last night was futile. I held her against me and savored the ease of her touch and the beauty of our similar passions.

214

It wasn't until we ran out of hot water that I remembered we didn't have a lifetime together ahead of us.

We quit the shower and Sydney ordered room service. I was ravenous by then. We devoured everything on the cart, including the crackers, and curled up together on the still unmade and thoroughly ravaged bed.

"I need to tell you something," Sydney said. "I . . . you know I haven't been with anyone in years."

"I didn't know. It doesn't show, darling," I said. My heart thumped painfully. I didn't want her to tell me that we couldn't see each other once we went back to Chicago.

"That's not what I meant," she said. "I've done things I'm not proud of."

"When you drank?"

She nodded.

"That's the past. You don't have to tell me anything." What I wanted to talk about was the future.

"If I don't, someone else will. If not here, then when we get home."

Her words gave me a glimmer of hope — she acted as if we would continue seeing each other.

"And I'll know that it doesn't matter. You had affairs. I saw Patrice. I know there were others."

She sighed. "I didn't sleep around a little, Faith. I'm . . . this is going to shock you." She said, all in a rush, "I slept with at least three hundred women in the space of three years. I was in and out of bed sometimes twice a day and never with the same woman twice. The more I did it, the more I drank. The more I drank, the more I did it. I slept with wives who wanted kicks, confused singles who wanted to give sex with a woman a try, and a lot of women who hoped they would be the one I'd stay with. I was insatiable, and I can't go anywhere in Chicago without running into someone I slept with once upon a time."

My mouth was dry. "Was it just drinking that made you so . . ."

"So much a slut?"

I flinched. "Don't, Syd."

"It's true. It's what I was. For a while. I slept with all those women because I could. I was no better than Magic Johnson, but I never caught anything. When I was finally sober enough to realize the risks I'd run, it was the first time I genuinely thanked God for anything."

"Is that why you've been alone ever since?"

She nodded. "When I last ran for office the story of my endless peccadilloes was floated around in the papers. And the only thing that shut my opponents up was that I'd been pure as a virgin ever since I got sober."

I turned my head so she couldn't see my face. "And now that's been compromised."

"It doesn't have to be," she said. "Look at me."

I raised my gaze to hers, and the velvet brown engulfed me.

"I don't want to have an affair with you, Faith. I want more. I kept thinking that if I gave in to wanting you that I'd give in to all the other things I'd given in to. But it didn't happen. I didn't walk around this morning scheming how I'd get my next woman in bed. I didn't wish I had a little flask of

Glen in my breast pocket. All I could think about was coming back to you. About how I could possibly convince you to live with me."

My ears were ringing and I felt as if my heart would explode. "What about Eric?"

"I know," she said. "I hope you're right about how he felt. We'll have to see him together. That is, if you want me. Forever." Unbelievably, she didn't seem to know what I would say. The strong woman I held in my arms, who always seemed to me to know what she wanted and how she would get it, looked scared.

"Forever," I echoed. I leaned into her, raising my mouth to hers. "I want longer than forever."

Sydney looked at her watch, then at Alan Stevens. "Is he going to keep us waiting much longer?" She hadn't thought this interview was necessary and didn't intend to let Mark O'Leary make her feel like hired help by keeping her waiting.

Faith shifted in her chair, and Sydney keenly felt the nervousness Faith was trying to hide.

Alan shrugged. "We don't have to wait."

"Five minutes," Sydney said. "And then we'll leave."

After four minutes had elapsed the door of the inner office opened. "Alan," Mark boomed, "good to see you." He flicked a glance at Sydney and then Faith but didn't acknowledge their presence beyond a gesture that indicated they should all follow him inside.

217

Once they were settled in chairs and Mark behind his massive desk, Sydney said, "I asked for this meeting —"

"I've got a bone to pick with you," Mark said, interrupting her. He pointed at Faith with his cigar. "That's the bone."

Sydney wanted to bridle, but she didn't. She felt a surge of pride as Faith lifted her chin and gave Mark a calm but intent stare. Eric had been so right when he'd compared Faith to Eleanor of Aquitaine. Faith still protested the comparison; she would never see how regal she became when the Mark O'Learys of the world were crude.

"I've never been referred to as a bone before," Faith said. "Certainly not by someone who doesn't know me." She stood up and leaned over Mark's desk with her hand out. "I'm Faith Fitzgerald, Mr. O'Leary. It's a pleasure to meet you."

For a long moment, Sydney thought Mark would refuse to shake Faith's hand. Then he put down the cigar and gravely shook it. Faith sat down again and looked serene as always.

"As you can see," Sydney said, "Ms. Fitzgerald is not a bone."

"I was speaking metaphorically, and you know it," Mark said sourly. "You promised me no sex scandals, and I have it on good authority that you and she holed up in a hotel for a couple of days in San Francisco. And that she's moved in with you."

Sydney pressed her lips together and took a deep breath. The old goat. "Does your good authority also report that Ms. Fitzgerald has been welcomed into my family, in fact was a part of the family Christmas this year? That one of my uncles conducted a ceremony for us and that we've exchanged rings?"

"Did she sign a pre-nup?" Mark chewed on the end of his cigar and turned to Faith. "How much of the hundred million will you get when you break up?"

"We won't be breaking up, Mr. O'Leary." Faith's voice was so calm that Sydney felt steadied.

Mark grunted into his cigar and fixed his gaze on Sydney again. "And now all those voters are going to congratulate you on the nice little wifey? The times haven't changed that much."

"Maybe not," Sydney said. "But I still feel that my life can bear scrutiny, and so can Faith's."

"And voters are happier with married candidates," Alan said.

"They ain't really married," Mark said. "It's not possible."

"All things are possible to those who believe," Faith said. "Why sometimes I've believed as many as six impossible things before breakfast."

"The New Testament and Lewis Carroll," Sydney said.

Mark glared at both of them. "I'm glad you think this is funny."

"What are we supposed to think?" Sydney straightened in her chair. "Mark, I can win this election. I don't think that because I now have an intelligent, charming, wonderful woman in my life, whom I do not intend to hide in any way, of whom I am very proud, and whose love has made me properly humble —"

"That'll be the day —" Mark muttered.

"I don't think I've broken any promise I made to you. I certainly haven't broken any promises I made to myself. I'm not a married man running around on a yacht called Monkey Business with some floozy. All I want to know is what you're going to do about supporting my candidacy."

Alan shifted uneasily. He had warned Sydney against giving Mark any opening to back out of his support.

"What am I supposed to do about it?" Mark examined the end of his cigar. "I'm not going to dance in the streets because the dyke I've been telling everyone could beat the pants off the other side is flaunting her sex life in everyone's face."

"That's simply not true —"

"You don't have to convince me of anything," Mark said. "I'm only one vote. You being a dyke is going to become the center of this campaign — instead of any issues you might have wanted to discuss."

"Maybe it will. And maybe it won't." Sydney stood up, and Faith rose to her feet as well. "I just want to know what you plan to do."

"I'm going to wait and see your poll numbers, that's what I'm going to do."

Alan Stevens got to his feet. "Don't wait too long, Mark. It'd be the first time in twenty years a Democratic senator won without you."

Faith held out her hand. "It's been a pleasure, Mr. O'Leary."

Sydney watched in amazement as Mark O'Leary stood up and shook Faith's hand. "The pleasure's been all mine," he said without a trace of mockery. He looked at Sydney. "At least she's got balls."

"Ovaries, Mark," Sydney said. "She's got ovaries."

After our meeting with O'Leary, Sydney threw herself completely into arranging and assembling her press packets and materials to announce her candidacy. I had never considered how extensive this preparatory stage was. She developed small brochures that explained her views on public housing, access to health care, a woman's right to choose, biannual zero-based budgeting for all social programs, and on and on. When I wasn't teaching or delving through research, I found myself frequently in the role of final editor.

Our lives had melted together as easily as butter into toast. I had moved out of my apartment and Michael, recovering speedily from the final skin grafts, had moved in. Eric, once recovered from the shock of our announcement, began congratulating himself for having brought us together and had even gone so far as to say that if either of us made the other unhappy, we'd have him to reckon with. Meg loved to bring David for playtime in the spa. From my parents I heard nothing.

We put one of the unused rooms in Sydney's flat to good use by creating a study for me. My first week in it I sorted and arranged my research material and the second I actually began writing *Eleanor*. More often than not, however, I took my laptop into

Sydney's study — the room where I'd first realized that she was a wild, dangerous woman — and soaked up the fire while Duchess studiously ignored me.

There was one topic that we hadn't come to any resolution on: money. When I brought it up, Sydney evaded. The flat was paid for so I had no rent money to contribute. The marvelous Lucy, who fussed over me like a mother hen, and her housekeeping expenses were paid directly by Sydney's money manager, and Sydney had looked at me blankly when I said I wanted to pay my share of the grocery bill. I had wanted to have some sort of pre-nuptial agreement, but Sydney wouldn't hear of it, saying shortly that she didn't want to talk about failure.

I wasn't without my own resources, but they paled next to hers. I was only beginning to suspect how much. I didn't have an Aquitaine to balance against her empire. I didn't want people to think what Mark O'Leary had insinuated, that I was after the life of wealth and ease that Sydney could easily support. I had tried to talk to her about it, but she had been deliberately obtuse.

I was tapping my latest royalty check on my laptop when Sydney came in, flushed from her shower and wrapped in the white chenille robe I found absolutely delectable. "I'm still selling," I said, holding out the check.

She glanced at it and then said, "Congratulations, darling." She dropped a kiss on the top of my head and sat down in front of the fire. "Just wait until *Eleanor* hits the shelves."

"Syd, what did O'Leary mean by a hundred million?"

Her indulgent smile faded. "I suppose he was guessing at how much I'm worth."

"Was he far off?" Now that I'd ruined her mood, I decided to persist.

"Way off," she said.

There was a long silence, and then I said, "Why don't you want to talk about it? I told you I'd sign anything you thought was fair."

"I don't want to even consider that our relationship isn't going to last."

"Is that the real reason?" I gave her a long, steady look.

"I didn't want you to know how much," she said sullenly. "I was afraid your virtuous little heart would be appalled and you'd get cold feet."

I did feel a nervous flutter in my heart. "Appalled by what?"

Sydney sighed. "O'Leary wasn't just way off. He was way low. I've got more money than anyone could possibly spend in a lifetime. It just sits around in banks and blind trusts making me more money all the time. I have to use the blind trusts so I don't accidentally or intentionally benefit from legislation I have influence over. I have no idea what it's invested in. I just know there's more at the end of the year than at the beginning. It's rather scary. I try to give it away, but it just keeps growing."

"Maybe I don't want to know the numbers," I said. I was having trouble conceptualizing. "I just, well, people will talk."

"Yes, they will. Let them. I know you didn't marry me for my money, sweetheart."

"How so?" She was smiling at me and I found myself smiling back.

"Eric is a boy —"

"I noticed. If he weren't a boy there's no telling where I'd be now." I ducked the pillow she threw at me. Duchess raised her head, scandalized.

"And boys get left more money than girls, it's a fact of life. Eric started off with more than I'll ever have. And I don't actively invest my money, but Eric does. Whatever I have he's got twice that and then some." She crossed the room to kiss me lightly on the lips. "If you really wanted money, my dear little Eleanor, you'd have stayed in France."

Epilog

Entreat me not to leave thee, or to return from following after thee: for whither thou goest, I will go; and where thou lodgest, I will lodge: thy people shall be my people, and thy God my God: Where thou diest, will I die, and there will I be buried.
— Ruth to Naomi, RUTH 1:16-17

Carrie put her finger under my chin and nodded approvingly. "You look fine, dear. Don't be nervous." She smiled at me sweetly, then went to stand next to Eric senior. I took a deep breath and looked out into the sea of lights and cameras. I knew some of them were already filming.

"I guess we'll get started." The chair of the Illinois Democratic party, to whom I had just been introduced, rapped the podium microphone. "Thank you for coming, ladies and gentleman of the press, and to all the rest of you. This is an exciting day for the Democratic party because we are announcing the candidacy of Sydney Van Allen for state senate. I know this wasn't unexpected because the good sense of it has occurred to a great many people. I'm going to turn everything over to Ms. Van Allen, who will make some remarks and then detail her agenda to you. Copies of her speech are available at the table in the rear of the room, along with an exhaustive financial disclosure. I want to point out the financial disclosure is completely voluntary since Ms. Van Allen isn't accepting any public monies. Ladies and gentlemen, the candidate with no secrets, Sydney Van Allen."

The room erupted with the cheers of the many supporters who had packed the room and were giving the press conference a festive air.

Sydney stepped to the microphone and smiled confidently. When the applause and cheering continued she looked a little abashed, then raised her hands to quiet the room. It took several tries.

"Thank you, that's very encouraging," she said, with a radiant smile. "Before I go on, I want to introduce everyone here with me on the podium. I couldn't be better blessed with family and friends. Beginning at the left," she said with a gesture, "is my aunt, the Honorable Emily Van Allen, my cousin Terrence Downing and his wife, Dr. Judith Downing. Next to her is my Uncle Paul Van Allen, and his son, my cousin, the Honorable Paul Van Allen. Next to Paul is columnist Gemini Van Allen, my cousin, and these two wonderful people next to me are my parents, Caroline and Eric. In particular, without their love and support I would not be standing here today."

I swallowed nervously, then lifted my chin and thought how often Eleanor must have waited patiently at Louis's or Henry's side, aware that potentially hostile eyes were on her and that she couldn't cough or fidget. I thought that if there was a video clip on the evening news there was an excellent chance of my parents seeing me in the frame with Sydney. Just to the left of the last camera I could see Michael in his dress navy whites, hat tucked formally under his arm. Next to him, Meg beamed at me.

"On my right is my aunt, Representative Jane Saunders, and her husband, Richard Saunders. Next to Richard is my cousin, writer Madeline Sheele, my uncle The Reverend John Van Allen, and my dear, dear brother, Eric Van Allen."

She gave him that same gesture of homage he'd given to her at the Roebuck Award ceremony. It seemed so long ago. I looked up at him for a moment and found him winking at me.

"And closest to me of all," she said, her voice trembling ever so slightly as she put her arm around me, "my partner and love of my life, Faith Fitzgerald."

Her arm was trembling, and I smiled at her with my heart in my eyes.

It was done. We had arrived, together, on the shores of our future. The rest, as they say, would be history.

Author's Note

I am not Catholic (nor a member of any organized religion for that matter) and therefore relied on the expert help of several Catholic and recovering Catholic friends. However, if any inaccuracies remain in my portrayal of Catholicism, they are purely of my making and I do apologize. Thank you J&P and C&M for your attention to detail.

Many faiths teach that homosexuality is an abomination — any church choosing to adopt Leviticus 19:22 (or the nearly verbatim restatement in Leviticus 20:13) as a part of its doctrine teaches lesbians and gay men that they are not worthy of religion's rewards. In addition to telling a story that delights my readers and affirms our lives, I hoped to illuminate the spiritual cost of denial and hate. I continue to have faith that people can change.

Faith is the substance of things hoped for, the evidence of things not seen.

— HEBREWS 11:1

About the Author

Karin Kallmaker admits that her first crush on a woman was the local librarian. Just remembering the pencil through the loose, attractive bun makes her warm. Maybe it was the librarian's influence, but for whatever reason, at the age of 16, Karin fell into the arms of her first and only sweetheart.

There's a certain symmetry to the fact that ten years later, after seeing the film *Desert Hearts*, her sweetheart descended on the Berkeley Public Library to find some of "those" books. "Rule, Jane" led to "Lesbianism—Fiction" and then on to book after self-affirming book by and about lesbians. These books were the encouragement Karin needed to forget the so-called "mainstream" and spin her first romance for lesbians. That manuscript became her first novel, *In Every Port*.

The happily-ever-after couple, mated since 1977, now lives in the San Francisco Bay Area, and became Mom and Moogie to Kelson in 1995 and Eleanor in 1997.

All of Karin's work can now be found at Bella Books. Details and background about her novels, and her other pen name, Laura Adams, can be found at her own website.

Publications from
BELLA BOOKS, INC.
The best in contemporary lesbian fiction

P.O. Box 10543, Tallahassee, FL 32302
Phone: 800-729-4992
www.bellabooks.com

WILD THINGS by Karin Kallmaker. 228 pp. Dutiful daughter Faith has met the perfect man. There's just one problem: she's in love with his sister.   ISBN 1-931513-64-3 $12.95

SHARED WINDS by Kenna White. 216 pp. Can Emma rebuild more than just Lanny's marina?   ISBN 1-59493-006-6 $12.95

THE UNKNOWN MILE by Jaime Clevenger. 253 pp. Kelly's world is getting more and more complicated every moment.   ISBN 1-931513-57-0 $12.95

TREASURED PAST by Linda Hill. 189 pp. A shared passion for antiques leads to love.   ISBN 1-59493-003-1 $12.95

SIERRA CITY by Gerri Hill. 284 pp. Chris and Jesse cannot deny their growing attraction . . .   ISBN 1-931513-98-8 $12.95

ALL THE WRONG PLACES by Karin Kallmaker. 174 pp. Sex and the single girl—Brandy is looking for love and usually she finds it. Karin Kallmaker's first *After Dark* erotic novel.   ISBN 1-931513-76-7 $12.95

WHEN THE CORPSE LIES A Motor City Thriller by Therese Szymanski. 328 pp. Butch bad-girl Brett Higgins is used to waking up next to beautiful women she hardly knows. Problem is, this one's dead.   ISBN 1-931513-74-0 $12.95

GUARDED HEARTS by Hannah Rickard. 240 pp. Someone's reminding Alyssa about her secret past, and then she becomes the suspect in a series of burglaries.   ISBN 1-931513-99-6 $12.95

ONCE MORE WITH FEELING by Peggy J. Herring. 184 pp. Lighthearted, loving, romantic adventure.   ISBN 1-931513-60-0 $12.95

TANGLED AND DARK A Brenda Strange Mystery by Patty G. Henderson. 240 pp. When investigating a local death, Brenda finds two possible killers—one diagnosed with Multiple Personality Disorder.   ISBN 1-931513-75-9 $12.95

WHITE LACE AND PROMISES by Peggy J. Herring. 240 pp. Maxine and Betina realize sex may not be the most important thing in their lives.   ISBN 1-931513-73-2 $12.95

UNFORGETTABLE by Karin Kallmaker. 288 pp. Can Rett find love with the cheerleader who broke her heart so many years ago?   ISBN 1-931513-63-5 $12.95

HIGHER GROUND by Saxon Bennett. 280 pp. A delightfully complex reflection of the successful, high society lives of a small group of women. ISBN 1-931513-69-4 $12.95

LAST CALL A Detective Franco Mystery by Baxter Clare. 240 pp. Frank overlooks all else to try to solve a cold case of two murdered children . . . ISBN 1-931513-70-8 $12.95

ONCE UPON A DYKE: NEW EXPLOITS OF FAIRY-TALE LESBIANS by Karin Kallmaker, Julia Watts, Barbara Johnson & Therese Szymanski. 320 pp. You've never read fairy tales like these before! From Bella After Dark. ISBN 1-931513-71-6 $14.95

FINEST KIND OF LOVE by Diana Tremain Braund. 224 pp. Can Molly and Carolyn stop clashing long enough to see beyond their differences? ISBN 1-931513-68-6 $12.95

DREAM LOVER by Lyn Denison. 188 pp. A soft, sensuous, romantic fantasy.
 ISBN 1-931513-96-1 $12.95

NEVER SAY NEVER by Linda Hill. 224 pp. A classic love story . . . where rules aren't the only things broken. ISBN 1-931513-67-8 $12.95

PAINTED MOON by Karin Kallmaker. 214 pp. Stranded together in a snowbound cabin, Jackie and Leah's lives will never be the same. ISBN 1-931513-53-8 $12.95

WIZARD OF ISIS by Jean Stewart. 240 pp. Fifth in the exciting Isis series.
 ISBN 1-931513-71-4 $12.95

WOMAN IN THE MIRROR by Jackie Calhoun. 216 pp. Josey learns to love again, while her niece is learning to love women for the first time. ISBN 1-931513-78-3 $12.95

SUBSTITUTE FOR LOVE by Karin Kallmaker. 200 pp. When Holly and Reyna meet the combination adds up to pure passion. But what about tomorrow? ISBN 1-931513-62-7 $12.95

GULF BREEZE by Gerri Hill. 288 pp. Could Carly really be the woman Pat has always been searching for? ISBN 1-931513-97-X $12.95

THE TOMSTOWN INCIDENT by Penny Hayes. 184 pp. Caught between two worlds, Eloise must make a decision that will change her life forever. ISBN 1-931513-56-2 $12.95

MAKING UP FOR LOST TIME by Karin Kallmaker. 240 pp. Discover delicious recipes for romance by the undisputed mistress. ISBN 1-931513-61-9 $12.95

THE WAY LIFE SHOULD BE by Diana Tremain Braund. 173 pp. With which woman will Jennifer find the true meaning of love? ISBN 1-931513-66-X $12.95

BACK TO BASICS: A BUTCH/FEMME ANTHOLOGY edited by Therese Szymanski—from Bella After Dark. 324 pp. ISBN 1-931513-35-X $14.95

SURVIVAL OF LOVE by Frankie J. Jones. 236 pp. What will Jody do when she falls in love with her best friend's daughter? ISBN 1-931513-55-4 $12.95

LESSONS IN MURDER by Claire McNab. 184 pp. 1st Detective Inspector Carol Ashton Mystery. ISBN 1-931513-65-1 $12.95

DEATH BY DEATH by Claire McNab. 167 pp. 5th Denise Cleever Thriller.
 ISBN 1-931513-34-1 $12.95

CAUGHT IN THE NET by Jessica Thomas. 188 pp. A wickedly observant story of mystery, danger, and love in Provincetown. ISBN 1-931513-54-6 $12.95

DREAMS FOUND by Lyn Denison. Australian Riley embarks on a journey to meet her birth mother . . . and gains not just a family, but the love of her life.
ISBN 1-931513-58-9 $12.95

A MOMENT'S INDISCRETION by Peggy J. Herring. 154 pp. Jackie is torn between her better judgment and the overwhelming attraction she feels for Valerie.
ISBN 1-931513-59-7 $12.95

IN EVERY PORT by Karin Kallmaker. 224 pp. Jessica has a woman in every port. Will meeting Cat change all that?
ISBN 1-931513-36-8 $12.95

TOUCHWOOD by Karin Kallmaker. 240 pp. Rayann loves Louisa. Louisa loves Rayann. Can the decades between their ages keep them apart?
ISBN 1-931513-37-6 $12.95

WATERMARK by Karin Kallmaker. 248 pp. Teresa wants a future with a woman whose heart has been frozen by loss. Sequel to *Touchwood*.
ISBN 1-931513-38-4 $12.95

EMBRACE IN MOTION by Karin Kallmaker. 240 pp. Has Sarah found lust or love?
ISBN 1-931513-39-2 $12.95

ONE DEGREE OF SEPARATION by Karin Kallmaker. 232 pp. Sizzling small town romance between Marian, the town librarian, and the new girl from the big city.
ISBN 1-931513-30-9 $12.95

CRY HAVOC A Detective Franco Mystery by Baxter Clare. 240 pp. A dead hustler with a headless rooster in his lap sends Lt. L.A. Franco headfirst against Mother Love.
ISBN 1-931513931-7 $12.95

DISTANT THUNDER by Peggy J. Herring. 294 pp. Bankrobbing drifter Cordy awakens strange new feelings in Leo in this romantic tale set in the Old West.
ISBN 1-931513-28-7 $12.95

COP OUT by Claire McNab. 216 pp. 4th Detective Inspector Carol Ashton Mystery.
ISBN 1-931513-29-5 $12.95

BLOOD LINK by Claire McNab. 159 pp. 15th Detective Inspector Carol Ashton Mystery. Is Carol unwittingly playing into a deadly plan?
ISBN 1-931513-27-9 $12.95

TALK OF THE TOWN by Saxon Bennett. 239 pp. With enough beer, barbecue and B.S., anything is possible!
ISBN 1-931513-18-X $12.95

MAYBE NEXT TIME by Karin Kallmaker. 256 pp. Sabrina has everything she ever wanted—except Jorie.
ISBN 1-931513-26-0 $12.95

WHEN GOOD GIRLS GO BAD: A Motor City Thriller by Therese Szymanski. 230 pp. Brett, Randi, and Allie join forces to stop a serial killer.   ISBN 1-931513-11-2 $12.95

A DAY TOO LONG: A Helen Black Mystery by Pat Welch. 328 pp. This time Helen's fate is in her own hands.
ISBN 1-931513-22-8 $12.95

THE RED LINE OF YARMALD by Diana Rivers. 256 pp. The Hadra's only hope lies in a magical red line . . . climactic sequel to *Clouds of War*.   ISBN 1-931513-23-6 $12.95

OUTSIDE THE FLOCK by Jackie Calhoun. 224 pp. Jo embraces her new love and life.
ISBN 1-931513-13-9 $12.95

LEGACY OF LOVE by Marianne K. Martin. 224 pp. Read the whole Sage Bristo story.
ISBN 1-931513-15-5 $12.95

STREET RULES: A Detective Franco Mystery by Baxter Clare. 304 pp. Gritty, fast-paced mystery with compelling Detective L.A. Franco ISBN 1-931513-14-7 $12.95

RECOGNITION FACTOR: 4th Denise Cleever Thriller by Claire McNab. 176 pp. Denise Cleever tracks a notorious terrorist to America. ISBN 1-931513-24-4 $12.95

NORA AND LIZ by Nancy Garden. 296 pp. Lesbian romance by the author of *Annie on My Mind*. ISBN 1931513-20-1 $12.95

MIDAS TOUCH by Frankie J. Jones. 208 pp. Sandra had everything but love. ISBN 1-931513-21-X $12.95

BEYOND ALL REASON by Peggy J. Herring. 240 pp. A romance hotter than Texas. ISBN 1-9513-25-2 $12.95

ACCIDENTAL MURDER: 14th Detective Inspector Carol Ashton Mystery by Claire McNab. 208 pp. Carol Ashton tracks an elusive killer. ISBN 1-931513-16-3 $12.95

SEEDS OF FIRE: Tunnel of Light Trilogy, Book 2 by Karin Kallmaker writing as Laura Adams. 274 pp. In Autumn's dreams no one is who they seem. ISBN 1-931513-19-8 $12.95

DRIFTING AT THE BOTTOM OF THE WORLD by Auden Bailey. 288 pp. Beautifully written first novel set in Antarctica. ISBN 1-931513-17-1 $12.95

CLOUDS OF WAR by Diana Rivers. 288 pp. Women unite to defend Zelindar! ISBN 1-931513-12-0 $12.95

DEATHS OF JOCASTA: 2nd Micky Knight Mystery by J.M. Redmann. 408 pp. Sexy and intriguing Lambda Literary Award-nominated mystery. ISBN 1-931513-10-4 $12.95

LOVE IN THE BALANCE by Marianne K. Martin. 256 pp. The classic lesbian love story, back in print! ISBN 1-931513-08-2 $12.95

THE COMFORT OF STRANGERS by Peggy J. Herring. 272 pp. Lela's work was her passion . . . until now. ISBN 1-931513-09-0 $12.95

WHEN EVIL CHANGES FACE: A Motor City Thriller by Therese Szymanski. 240 pp. Brett Higgins is back in another heart-pounding thriller. ISBN 0-9677753-3-7 $11.95

CHICKEN by Paula Martinac. 208 pp. Lynn finds that the only thing harder than being in a lesbian relationship is ending one. ISBN 1-931513-07-4 $11.95

TAMARACK CREEK by Jackie Calhoun. 208 pp. An intriguing story of love and danger. ISBN 1-931513-06-6 $11.95

DEATH BY THE RIVERSIDE: 1st Micky Knight Mystery by J.M. Redmann. 320 pp. Finally back in print, the book that launched the Lambda Literary Award-winning Micky Knight mystery series. ISBN 1-931513-05-8 $11.95

EIGHTH DAY: A Cassidy James Mystery by Kate Calloway. 272 pp. In the eighth installment of the Cassidy James mystery series, Cassidy goes undercover at a camp for troubled teens. ISBN 1-931513-04-X $11.95

MIRRORS by Marianne K. Martin. 208 pp. Jean Carson and Shayna Bradley fight for a future together. ISBN 1-931513-02-3 $11.95

THE ULTIMATE EXIT STRATEGY: A Virginia Kelly Mystery by Nikki Baker. 240 pp. The long-awaited return of the wickedly observant Virginia Kelly. ISBN 1-931513-03-1 $11.95

FOREVER AND THE NIGHT by Laura DeHart Young. 224 pp. Desire and passion ignite the frozen Arctic in this exciting sequel to the classic romantic adventure *Love on the Line*.
ISBN 0-931513-00-7 $11.95

WINGED ISIS by Jean Stewart. 240 pp. The long-awaited sequel to *Warriors of Isis* and the fourth in the exciting Isis series.
ISBN 1-931513-01-5 $11.95

ROOM FOR LOVE by Frankie J. Jones. 192 pp. Jo and Beth must overcome the past in order to have a future together.
ISBN 0-9677753-9-6 $11.95

THE QUESTION OF SABOTAGE by Bonnie J. Morris. 144 pp. A charming, sexy tale of romance, intrigue, and coming of age.
ISBN 0-9677753-8-8 $11.95

SLEIGHT OF HAND by Karin Kallmaker writing as Laura Adams. 256 pp. A journey of passion, heartbreak, and triumph that reunites two women for a final chance at their destiny.
ISBN 0-9677753-7-X $11.95

MOVING TARGETS: A Helen Black Mystery by Pat Welch. 240 pp. Helen must decide if getting to the bottom of a mystery is worth hitting bottom.
ISBN 0-9677753-6-1 $11.95

CALM BEFORE THE STORM by Peggy J. Herring. 208 pp. Colonel Robicheaux retires from the military and comes out of the closet.
ISBN 0-9677753-1-0 $11.95

OFF SEASON by Jackie Calhoun. 208 pp. Pam threatens Jenny and Rita's fledgling relationship.
ISBN 0-9677753-0-2 $11.95

BOLD COAST LOVE by Diana Tremain Braund. 208 pp. Jackie Claymont fights for her reputation and the right to love the woman she chooses.
ISBN 0-9677753-2-9 $11.95

THE WILD ONE by Lyn Denison. 176 pp. Rachel never expected that Quinn's wild yearnings would change her life forever.
ISBN 0-9677753-4-5 $11.95

SWEET FIRE by Saxon Bennett. 224 pp. Welcome to Heroy—the town with more lesbians per capita than any other place on the planet!
ISBN 0-9677753-5-3 $11.95